Flow

Lief Achten

Copyright © 2012 by Lief Achten

Translated from 'Vloeibaar', by Lief Achten

Por el cuerpo volvemos al comienzo,
espiral de quietud y movimiento.

Sabor, saber mortal, pausa finita,
tiene principio y fin -y es sin medida.

La noche entra y nos cubre su marea;
repite el mar sus sílabas, ya negras.

We return to the very start,
Through our body,
Spiral of motion and rest.
A knowing flavour of mortality,
Immeasurable respite,
With an ending and beginning.
Night comes,
Its tide covers us.
The sea repeats its syllables
Black already.

Octavio Paz

For N.

Part 1

I can take the despair. It's the hope I can't stand.

Clockwise, Brian Stimpson

When I met her, I was struck by two things: her resolve and her eyes. Ayane was driven, practical and used to delegating, someone great to have around in a crisis. We attended the same prenatal yoga class – she was in her nineteenth week, I was in my fourteenth. Collecting a mat at the back of the room I bent over and felt suddenly unwell. Just before the world around me turned black, I felt her firm dancer's arms breaking my fall. When I came to, my head was leaning against her plump little bump while she was handing out instructions in a clipped, Japanese accent. I looked into her flat, keen eyes; up close she looked even more like an oriental mermaid. Her eyes were like buttons – smart, oval buttons of marbled bone.

'It's all right, I'm fine now.' I tried to escape her grip, but she held me tight. Ayane smelled faintly musky, dark and heavy and although I was starting to feel better, I wanted to curl around her comforting little orb of a belly with my head against her mini-bosom. *Night night, sleep tight.* She was the kind of mother I wanted to be, warm, strong and earthy - and in control.

Minutes later one of my sleeves was rolled up and someone took my blood pressure. Where had this man come from? When I looked up I was surprised to see Raf rushing into the classroom. He knelt down by my side and studied my face. He looked worried.

'I'm parked nearby. You all right, Em? Is everything ok?' His eyes wandered to my belly and beyond. However weak I was feeling, that didn't escape me. His discreetly inquisitive eyes were trying to meet mine, as if he expected some explanation, a sign, a casual nod to put him at ease: *blimey, look at us, mother and child splayed all over the floor. Don't worry, sweetie, I'm a little faint, that's all, to be expected at thirteen weeks, that's right, we're getting there.* But the question was not whether *I* was all right. The question was whether I was losing blood, whether I had stomach cramps.

Although the pain I might be feeling wasn't the main concern either. Unless it was caused by contractions of my womb as it was in the process of rejecting yet another foetus.

Raf and I had never seriously considered children, but as soon as we found out that we couldn't have any, we thought of little else. On the night of Raf's thirty-fifth birthday party, during our slightly drunken love-making, we decided to start a family. The idea just came to us and felt right. Raf already had a seven-year-old daughter from his previous marriage. I was thirty-four, had travelled and had dabbled in many a casual relationship; now I realised I was ready to settle down. For the first time in my life I felt secure enough in a relationship to have a child. Expressions which would later come back to haunt me: 'starting a family' and 'to have a child'. As if this was merely a decision fuelled by determination and willpower or worse, belief. *You have to believe in it, Emma. Negative thoughts end up by fulfilling themselves.* It seemed having a child was the ultimate reward for genuine coupledom. As time went on, people around me no longer found safe terminology to refer to other people's pregnancies without ruffling my feathers. When it looked increasingly likely that this particular miracle would pass me by, the subject was shunned entirely. When a conversation about a couple we knew suddenly dried up and the topic was changed, I knew enough. At the same time, it became an obsession; I was fascinated by pregnant women and other people's desire to have children, as if I wanted to pour salt into the wound: to punish myself, to exorcise my demons? I had no idea.

However, we started the whole project like every other innocent couple, with the admirable aim of fusing the best of ourselves. It wasn't even a question of trying – that would come later. It was self-evident: we deserved this. As Ayane would whisper in my ear years later: 'Having a child, Em, is like getting to know your partner all over again, but in a much less threatening way.' She was a good friend; when she spoke those words of wisdom I was once again expecting and past the so-called critical phase – the marvel would soon reveal itself to me too.

Raf and I had been together for nearly four years. His little girl stayed with us every second weekend. We both enjoyed our time with Marie, who was crazy about her father but found it difficult to accept his divided attention. Raf's relationship with Nora, his ex, had not become any less sour over the years and their communication was openly hostile. He tried very hard to keep Marie away from the firing line, but Nora had no such compunctions; as the abandoned partner, without a new man in her life, her most effective means of revenge was to stir up animosity for her ex in Marie. The girl became her battle ground. We hoped and believed that a new baby would calm things down.

I suffered from endometriosis, a condition whereby cells from the lining of the uterus appear and flourish elsewhere in the abdominal cavity and form so-called chocolate cysts which, under the influence of female hormones, start to bleed and cause painful scar tissue. Some women were covered in cysts but didn't experience any negative side-effects. Others, like me, didn't show much evidence of the disease, but were often in agony. For some women it proved practically impossible to become pregnant. I was about to discover I was one of them. My first conception had been a fluke.

Apart from chocolate cysts, I turned out to be blessed with a heart-shaped womb; Raf couldn't possibly top that on Valentine's day. However, contrary to what the name suggested, this could form a significant obstacle to the reproductive aim of our intercourse, since a foetus prefers to attach itself to the upper part of the womb – which in my case was shielded off by an additional wall. Initially I saw a romantic side to it all: my baby would be growing in its very own heart-shaped, chocolate dotted home, reassured by the knowledge of being utterly wanted. Moreover, I was convinced that a foetus who wasn't held back by an obstruction in the womb had to be a tough little dude, which must bode well for the remainder of the pregnancy.

Raf and I decided not to be scared off by medical statistics and worst-case scenarios. 'Great, you can hand in your notice now, love, the job's done,' he joked after our first giddy night of unprotected sex. A month and a half later I embraced the good news. I peed on my first little stick, and although I was ecstatic when a blue line started to appear slowly but surely between my trembling fingers, I hadn't really expected anything else – my breasts had been painfully swollen for days. It made perfect sense. After all, we had eradicated the barriers between my ovaries and Raf's keen swimmers. I was experiencing what happens to all normal women: you make love and you have a baby. The undiluted delight of those initial weeks of my first pregnancy would never return. Although I suspect that I actually experienced more of a lazy sort of contentment - having reached this target, chanting my inner mantra: *'It's ok, it's nature's way'*. It was with hindsight that I labelled the initial surprise 'rapturous'. Whichever way you look at it, I should have enjoyed the wonderful glow of promise much more than I did. But it was precisely the absence of such pressures that made this carefree, quiet happiness so magical. Never again would I give myself so readily. Never again would I have such naïve faith in my body. Never again would I consider conception as a matter of course; not for me, not for a friend, not even for my cat.

I suppose our belief in the powers of the body works in much the same way as our awareness of our own mortality. Until things go wrong, we are complacent. We believe our bodies to be infallible. Until they fail us and we catch a glimpse of the end, this belief is blind.

It was a scorching day in July. We were in the car on our way to Ikea. Raf was driving and I was talking about the principles of *feng shui*. Suddenly I felt my knickers get wet; an intense, warm gush had unmistakably spilled onto the leather seat of our brand-new Audi TT - an expensive toy for which Raf's justification had been our expanding family. Initially I continued to talk while I quietly moved my hand underneath my skirt to my underwear.
'And yet, I do understand what they mean by blocked energy.'
There is a difference between suspecting and knowing. As long as I continued to talk, I could keep the latter at bay. After all, this could be any number of bodily fluids, right? – what did I know about pregnancies? Bea, our GP, would no doubt soon put me at ease: 'It probably gave you a fright, didn't it? But it's perfectly normal, Emma. During the first weeks of a pregnancy, the cervix is lubricated in order to prepare the birth channel. Ingenious, isn't it?' But then I held up my bloody fingers, somewhat bashfully, as if I had sneezed and was waiting for someone to hand me a Kleenex.

'Emma?'

Raf was standing at the foot of my bed with a white orchid in a large pot. I liked orchids, albeit not especially white ones.

'Are you in pain?'

'No, not really. Is the baby...?'

I'm sorry. They have performed a D and C. You had a miscarriage, Em. An early one. It's not at all unusual, they say. It happens a lot with first pregnancies. In fact, it's even...'

'Raf, stop.' My head was filled with cotton wool and I wanted to slip back into the dullness of the anaesthetic and not think.'

'What?'

'Come here and sit with me for a while.' He put the orchid on the night stand, sat down on the bed and stroked the sheet that covered my belly. It was meant tenderly, but it struck me as confrontational. Raf was a pragmatist. A man of solutions, an action man, a hiker, a surfer and a handyman, a web designer. I loved him dearly, but secretly felt that he even approached our love-making as if it were one of his tasks. Funnily enough, the very things that annoyed me most were also those that attracted me to him: his lack of sentimentality, his toughness, his dry sense of humour. We were polar opposites, but perhaps this was what made us so resilient and enabled us, after every disappointment, to get up and start afresh. I appreciated Raf's no-nonsense approach; on the other hand, I felt isolated in my loss. I was a wavering mess.

Something had been taken from me. That's how it felt that first time.

However paradoxically, I felt emptier and more desolate after my first miscarriage than after my fifth. My husband, my doctor, Clearblue, my breasts – they were all part of the conspiracy.

After all, I had been promised something. I had been given a taster of it but then it had been snatched away abruptly. ('And, are you happy?' 'Yes, of course!' *Register: what am I feeling? Joy? Confusion? Excitement? Panic? Disbelief? Curiosity? Amazement?)* I hadn't even had the time to entertain the possibility of something going wrong. 'Be cautious, Emma,' a pregnant friend advised me. 'Try to contain your euphoria until week twelve.' Why? Dear God, such a fuss. I was pregnant - big deal. I was sincerely happy. Raf and I would soon be welcoming our child, and that was all there was to it.

And then there was no longer anything. No, worse still, there was *less.* Many years and losses later, my therapist would talk about grieving and loss. I felt loss and lost all right, but I was careful not to let it show – not wanting to appear melodramatic. I didn't think I had the right to such feelings after barely nine weeks of hope and a spark of life the size of a finger nail.

Raf determined the speed and tone of my recovery. "Chin up, girl. This is only a temporary setback and it's perfectly normal." I acquiesced, although the logic of it escaped me: death wasn't normal, there had barely been life.
'Why don't we plan that trip to Queensland? Book our flights. What do you think?' Some six months earlier we had been busy preparing a holiday to Australia, until we made a complete U-turn, decided to start a family and I became pregnant sooner than expected.

I realised that Raf was trying to cheer me up, but it felt forced. 'And if I become pregnant again in the meantime, Raf? Then what?' I was aware of my whining voice, I sounded like a spoiled child. 'Surely you can travel when you're pregnant, can't you?' It was a sincere question. I had never seen him so accommodating. 'I won't be travelling before week twelve, and during the final two months I definitely won't be going anywhere.'
'Well, can't we see how it goes? It all happened so fast the first time; I'll bet there's every chance of you conceiving quickly again. We could book the tickets after the three-month scan, couldn't we? Yes or yes?' He gave me an encouraging smile; next time everything would run smoothly. I pretended to cave in, hoping he would forget all about the trip once a baby was on the way.

Raf and I had met on Kangaroo Island in Southern Australia. The previous summer I had attended a jewellery design course in Ireland. The man running the course was a charming Dubliner who lived in Australia, where he had his own jewellery store and gallery in The Rocks. Sean and I had started an affair, which resulted in a more or less open invitation to visit him in Sydney. Two months in each other's company, even in Sydney's trendy Darlinghurst, proved more than enough. Sean was an incredibly funny, soulful man with an enormous drinking problem, which he trivialised with his dry, self-deprecating wit. We said our amicable goodbyes at Sydney airport, where I boarded a flight to Adelaide, from where I would travel to Cape Jervis to take the boat to Kangaroo Island. Initially, I stayed at the youth hostel in Penneshaw, where the ferries arrived. But after a few days I decided to rent a car with Tammy, a bossy, middle-aged New-Zealander, to explore the rest of the island.

Raf was staying in Stokes Bay on the island's North shore with his brother Tom, his sister-in-law Becky and their four-year-old girl. Tom and Becky lived and worked in Glenelg in Adelaide, and usually came to Kangaroo Island for Christmas. Raf had been divorced for about a year. He was close to his brother. They had always shared a passion for water sports and although the surf at Stokes was not spectacular, it was a good place for kayaking and sailing, and the rocks formed a shallow pool where it was safe for Bobby to play. It was an ideal holiday spot for the brothers, who hadn't seen each other in years. Tom and his family rented a cabin with ocean views high on the cliffs. Raf stayed, like Tammy and myself, in the campsite down at the bay. It seemed like paradise. Kangaroos and wallabies came bouncing out of their hiding places at nightfall and pelicans glided elegantly over the water. Every now and then a koala ventured out of the eucalyptus trees.

On New Year's Eve a party was organised in the campgrounds, without fireworks, out of consideration for the wildlife. Raf was responsible for the barbecue, and together with Tammy and Saskia, a young, blonde vamp who, like Raf, came from Amsterdam, I was asked to come up with silly games to play. We decided on the usual suspects, such as spin the bottle and truth or dare and charades, of course.
That evening, when we started to play charades, Raf and I turned out to be equally knowledgeable film buffs and our hints for more obscure, art house films were generally only deciphered by the other.
'One syllable.' I nodded.
'Sounds like?' Again, I nodded to the tanned Dutchman, who didn't appear to get drunk, as he grabbed yet another beer from the cool box. As a Belgian I didn't think much of Australian beer, but I secretly admired people who could keep on drinking without, to all appearances, getting drunk. According to Sean's theories, Raf was a novice drinker: after years of excess, increasingly less alcohol would be needed to reach the desired level of intoxication. In the light of what he was able to down in one session, I had found his logic questionable.
I pointed at Tammy's head. 'Red hair?' An Australian teenage girl raised her hand, as if she were in class. My hands fluttered through the air, clumsily trying to indicate that she was close. 'Ginger?' shouted the fat Fin. Delighted, I raised a thumb; like most contestants, lacking a voice, I had started to exaggerate all my gestures. Ostentatiously, I held up both index fingers, making the sign of a cross. 'Plus?' Saskia shouted enthusiastically,

as if she had just deciphered the Rosetta Stone. I gave her a measured nod and then started my second clue, pointing to my glass. 'Red wine?' His elongated *wine* had the ring of an Antwerp accent to it. I started to laugh but tried to do so silently. Everyone else, however, burst out in loud laughter. Joe from Brisbane, who had been snoring in his fold-up chair for some time, had suddenly woken up; perhaps he just wanted his glass topped up. Searching for a way to express 'half', I raised my left hand horizontally in front of me and held my right hand vertically underneath is. 'T?' I shook my head. 'Half?' I nodded approvingly to the schoolgirl. 'Wine. Ginger wine,' mumbled Raf, more to himself than to anyone else. As I looked at him expectantly I felt a smile spread across my lips. 'Go on! Oh, sorry. Forgive me!' I was nodding foolishly, with one hand in front of my mouth, realising I had broken the rules. Suddenly Raf jumped up energetically, pumped his fist in the air and landed in the sand in front of me. His eyes seemed just as shrewd and sober as earlier in the afternoon, when he had told to me with great fervour about the Ten Pound Poms having been shipped over from Britain to build a future in Australia after the war. His eyes burned into mine, as if, at any moment, he might ask me to marry him. I knew that he knew, and this, to my own astonishment, had become inexplicably important to me. 'Jindabyne!', he shouted triumphantly while he picked me up and whirled me around.

Ayane hardly ever used make-up, except for performances, and even then, minimally. She did not need it, if anything it distracted from her strong features. *'That's all right. After all, one mustn't tamper with perfection'*, one British director had remarked when she refused to go on stage with more than a dash of lippy. She had been contracted to the Royal Ballet of Flanders for many years. It was there she met her husband, who wasn't a dancer but a sound technician. When we met we felt our life stories somehow complemented each other's: she was a Dutch woman with a Fleming, I was a Fleming with a Dutch man. After all, Ayane, who had been three when she and her parents and siblings had traded Osaka for Den Hague, felt entirely Dutch, albeit with a strong pull from her oriental roots. We were both artists: she was a dancer, I was an actress and our respective husbands were convinced they kept us grounded and our arty whims in check.

Ayane was the very first girlfriend with whom I could literally share everything. We had more or less the same taste in clothes, shoes, accessories and interiors, which made shopping together a feast. We shared the same sort of surreal humour and both delighted in making the other one laugh; albeit often wryly as we were mercilessly honest with one another. When she held me in her strong grip that day in yoga, the prologue to my third miscarriage had set in. I did not yet know her name, she had only just picked up mine. Nonetheless, she was about to accompany me and Raf to the hospital and would be by my bedside when I woke up from yet another general anaesthetic. The dull awakening had become all too familiar. The mind clouded, heavy with eerie déjà vu. This rite of return from my own underworld felt like the struggle between disappointment and failure on one hand and the desire to return to the absolute stillness of the artificially induced sleep, on the other. My biggest fear had become my attraction to this big, black hole-of-nothingness, which was about to expel me. There was a strong call to give in and end the ultimate battle with hope. I hated coming to even more than I hated pain.
But this time was different. Ayane's complete lack of pep talk or fake empathy offered me a more liberating sound board for my grief than Raf and his family provided, alongside my own relatives and all of the friends and colleagues who suddenly came crawling out of the woodwork to suffocate me in commiserations. Women supporting other women in their hour of need: I never quite trusted them, justifiably or not, I always suspected a degree of triumph.

I thought she was asleep. Her breathing was slow and steady, her eyelids were closed, and her fingers were resting on the magazine in her lap. Suddenly a page was turned, Ayane shot a cursory glance in my direction.

'Emma, you're awake. It's me, Ayane'. It sounded like 'Aya! Naagh'. I wanted to reply with something witty but my head was too heavy. 'Of course, yes, Ayane, from pregnancy yoga', was all I managed.

'That's right, yes, from yoga.' It was my first encounter with Ayane's sensitivity.

'Try to get some more sleep.' She casually stroked my hand and returned to her silence. The magazine in her lap was closed as were her slanted eyes. It felt like she was sleeping next to me.

When I'm dead
I'll just be dead
I'll never have been a woman at all
Just a little girl

Claire Niveau, 'Dead Ringers'

Mothers with huge bags, mega bags, packed with baby stuff intrigued me, the bags more than anything. Bags with mums in parks and on trains, at the airport and at the swimming baths and at the doctors. Bags with mums on beaches and in elevators. Bags with mums visiting other mums. Dragging mums with massive bags full of alluring *stuff*, prepared for every whim, every need, every inconvenience imaginable of the child to be pacified. Had the divine provider's providence kicked in together with the FSH-hormone? I had started to wonder *if* or *how* I would ever know how to best fill such a bag. Would the design, the texture and colour of such a baby-essential-recipient still be a concern or would I have my priorities sorted out by then?
No one ever believed me when I said I longed for a universe in which my own needs and desires had become secondary.

Meanwhile I had four miscarriages behind me. After 'the product' of the second conception had been spontaneously aborted, as they say in medical terms, at ten weeks, Raf and I tried, for over a year to make a new baby, to no avail. At our wit's end we consulted the GP, who concurred with our urgent need to call in specialised fertility assistance.

Two failed IVF attempts later I was almost thirty-nine. The medics however, remained incredibly optimistic, almost more than optimistic. After all my reaction to the drugs in both IVF treatments had been very encouraging, indeed. I had managed to conceive, hadn't I? The mere fact that the embryo of respectively ten and nine week's gestation had been expelled, did not question the success of the treatment. *If it hadn't been for the child-unfriendly shape of this womb of yours, you'd most definitely had been a mother by now ma'am*, was how one of the consultants put it.

I was in too much pain to respond and had become oblivious to the numerous tactless *faux-pas*. When my second pregnancy had started to go wrong while Raf was in the Netherlands for a job, I had admitted myself to the Accident and Emergency department of our local hospital, after a taxi ride from hell. The locum, a young Greek consultant, informed me in broken Dutch there was no more heart beat but I needn't worry, he would make sure to dispose of 'the product' promptly. When he noticed the tears running down my cheeks he seemed puzzled and asked me what was the matter. 'I'm sad', I said. 'O yes, sad', he repeated, as if making a mental note to store the notion for future reference.

The doctors decided to surgically remove the septum which divided my uterus in two. Hopefully this reversal of my womb's heart shape would increase not only my chances to conceive, but to carry a pregnancy to term. However, during the operation it became clear that the hormones I had taken in order to stimulate my ovaries to produce more eggs, had more than tripled the so-called chocolate cysts and the endometriosis had now spread to my bowels. I carried my very own chocolate factory but it was no laughing matter, the pain was constant and worse than ever. The fact that I no longer seemed to register it was testament to my eagerness to please everyone, but more than that, to the price I was willing to pay to have a child. I was doubled up with pain and horrified by the prospect of more follicle stimulating hormone treatment. But luckily that wasn't an immediate worry. In order to shrink the endometriosis and relieve the pain I was told I could start a different type of hormone treatment, which would temporarily trick my body into the menopause, during which time I would be infertile and 'only' suffer from menopausal symptoms. I was confronted with an impossible dilemma: choosing to be free from pain and the worries about conceiving for a while was a tempting prospect put it meant I would be putting my fertile years on hold. Choosing to try for a baby implied physical and most likely mental agony too. I was stuck: I wanted quality of life and I wanted a child. At that point, regaining the former seemed more pressing. Subconsciously I must have secretly longed to get away from the fertility circus, albeit for a while, for I grabbed my chemical menopause with both hands.

Raf had never been willing to consider adoption or surrogacy, so I knew I had to ready my own body for potential further battles. In the end, with less endometrioses my chances to become pregnant would increase. And even though my body did not seem to share my obsession with pregnancy, at thirty-nine I entered the menopause with renewed militancy. I tolerated hot flushes, night sweats, sleeplessness and headaches and regarded Raf's romantic advances with the clinical distance of a sexual anthropologist.

By now, as an actress, I had been out of work for more than a year and a half. Two years earlier I had been regularly stopped in the street by people wanting a signature of 'Neeltje', my character in a popular Flemish youth series. Now I was a minor celebrity at best. For more serious work I was no longer approached either; after my first IVF-miscarriage I had needed to pull out of a production of Lorca's 'The house of Bernarda Alba', just when the company was about to embark on a tour of The Netherlands. My professional name was tainted.

I was fed up with my interim life.

It seemed for years I had been waiting for something to begin, as if all I did was a mere means to kill the time. I was fed up with myself, with sex on command, with my squabbles with Raf, with fertility clinics and my own worn out pain monologues and hysterical outbursts which invariably ended up with me, all wrung out, leaning on Ayane's ever available shoulder. And hope, I was especially fed up with hope.
And yet Raf and I continued to try and to dream and to long and did our best to erase distressing memories of past ordeals. We were whizzing round in circles on a carousel that we were unable to stop and those around us did nothing but increase the speed. The expensive doctors with their promising prognoses, who treated me with the respect afforded to a race horse on its way to ultimate victory, my sisters, my parents, all of whom showered us with hang-in-theres. My mother dreamt I was dancing on a roundabout with a small red-haired girl on my shoulders. Wasn't that a sign?

I had just turned forty when, after successful corrective surgery to my uterus, I was encouraged to try again. Our *last* chance. One final IVF attempt was what Raf and I had unanimously agreed on. Not only emotionally and physically were we finished, but financially too. We had re-mortgaged the house and borrowed a substantial amount of money from my mum and dad, which both of us were eager to pay back.
Raf was well paid, but we would not be able to live on one salary for much longer. I needed to return to work, acting parts or not, baby or no baby.

'Once I've finished in here I can do Marie's room with the big one, what do you reckon?'

'Sorry?'

Raf gesticulated wildly, his back facing me, his voice muffled by his dust mask. We had hired machines to sand the floor boards. He pulled down his mask and turned to face me. A grey film covered his hair. He wore thick heavy-duty gloves.

'I said that I ...'

'I know. Yes. I heard you. *Marie's* room next.' I stressed the girl's name.

'I thought you hadn't heard me.'

'I hadn't, but you are more than a bit predictable. We discuss something, we reach a compromise and then you just go and do your own thing, regardless.'

'What the hell are you talking about?' The mask and the gloves had been thrown on the bare boards. Raf ruffled through his hair, a haze of powder rose up. He looked at his hands, then at me through narrow eyes, he was buying time. If I hadn't known better I'd blame the dust for his cloudy eyes, but I sensed the storm ahead and felt oddly triumphant.

Was he right? Did I invariably feel the urge to spoil things between us, after a relatively peaceful stretch? Did I need these bouts of conflict, in order to vent my own pent up anger and frustration? Or was it he who was unreasonable and did I need to assert myself from time to time?

I was exhausted. Since last week's positive test result I had been walking on egg shells. I was pregnant, but didn't feel in the least bit thrilled. No longer could I count on Raf's empathy and who could blame him? He'd been through one too many emotional maelstroms.

'Listen, Raf.' I was walking towards him, feigning ignorance. I knew the time for civilised debate had expired and phase two had set in, that of callous provocation. I made big eyes, faking shock, when Raf raised his voice, or tried to.

'No, Emma, you listen for a change: I am utterly fed up with this, do you hear me? Marie is my daughter and I've more than had it with your infantile competitive battles! Do you hear me? Do you hear me?' Raf was skipping about on our messy boards, pointing and swaying his defenceless slender index finger, screeching in his unimposing falsetto, the one he kept for rows.

Raf's upset-voice sounded like a cartoon mouse, a sad contrast to his normal, attractive, masculine tone.

I was tempted to make a play on words with 'infantile', but that wouldn't have hit the spot.

'Hardly', I retaliated. 'Those minimalist shrieks barely carry.' My delivery was dry and sarcastic and the actress in me was revelling in the effect.

'Fucking cunt', he muttered under his breath and to my dismay that sounded exceptionally spiteful. He shot me a deadly glance, stormed off the stairs and slammed the front door shut.

Marie, now in her teens, had grown into an assertive goth with a jet black, a-symmetrical bob, copious amounts of makeup and braces. She still was the apple of her daddy's eye, but our baby perils hadn't done much for her bond with me. Six years earlier she had quietly tolerated my presence, now her attitude had moved to full blown hostility.

I understood only too well how the prospect of having to share her father with a brand-new half sibling threatened her position. What I could not stomach, however, was Raf's lack of loyalty towards me. It never felt he explicitly told her off when she was rude to me or hurtful. I suspected he was afraid to lose her affection and, although I did understand that, I felt his attitude was cowardly.

We had bought a period house in the heart of the city and had been renovating it for as long as I could remember. It had three bedrooms. We slept in the largest one, to the west. At the back of the house, facing south, was a second light and spacious room with a view on to the garden. It had always had the baby's name on it. It was the destination of the third bedroom we had never been able to agree on; it was a conversation we tended to avoid.

I wanted to make it into a multi-functional room, a space to be used both as study and guest room, an ideal space for Marie to hang out when she came to stay, although that occurred less and less. Raf wanted to make it clear to his daughter that she was always welcome and that she had her very own hideaway under our roof. I kept doggedly insisting she *did* have her own retreat in this room. Besides, where would we put up his brother when he came over or my sister who lived in Norway? Were we to shove them on to the sofa in the living room? Some welcome! This conversation, or rather the many hidden layers lurking underneath, became our Achilles heel. Marie's existence and Raf's reluctance to look into alternative ways to obtain a baby, were rapidly undermining our increasingly fragile bond.

'Have you eaten?' I nodded dreamily. Ayane poured me a big glass of cranberry juice, it looked tantalisingly like a glass of chilled rosé. She steadied the heavy glass carafe on the coffee table and started to extract an ice cube from an ingenious little metal cooler, with what looked like an antique pair of sugar pliers. Ayane and her gadgets. 'That's it? You're not going to offer me a drink?'

She came and sat down next to me and fixed me with a severe look, real or not, with her I could never be sure. My friend was expecting her second baby in the spring. Next week she would enter her third trimester. After my phone call with the IVF department last Wednesday, I had quickly calculated that, if all was going according to plan, at the time my friend would be having her baby, I myself would have reached the fifteen-week hurdle. This would be a point in time of potential dilemma, if an amniocentesis were to be called for. I suspected that my obsession with such calculations was a substitute for the overconfidence of my first pregnancy. Now there was pressure with every advancing week. If ever I would be lucky enough to reach week thirteen, it would feel less like a victory than a new ordeal.

I had become addicted to saving up my happiness-vouchers. I wondered if I would ever be able to enjoy cashing them in, if I ever hit the jackpot. Delayed gratification? As a child I had had a neurotic aunt with whom I went to stay, every once in a while. She had no children of her own, but according to my mother she was itching to spoil my sister and me. Oh, and she would... if first the dishes were done and the floor was mopped then-oh-then she would, cosily curled up under the blanket, with toffee popcorn and Fanta enjoy *The children on Seacrow Island*. But by such time there would inevitably be more pressing breadcrumbs or urgent dust-traps that made her restless and before I knew, it would be bedtime and once again too late for *Boatsman* en *Skrållan*. Curled up on the settee with aunty B remained a mirage. I sometimes feared I would become just like her the day my baby became a reality. Would the countless fears, endured by every mother, eternally overshadow my happiness? Sometimes I felt my desire was no more than a form of indignation about motherhood denied. Sometimes I even believed the bastards who were trying to console me with their *perhaps it's for the best.*

My life seemed to consist of a succession of menstrual cycles and pregnancy stages and not just mine at that: new colleagues and friends would be subtly quizzed about their interest in starting a family. Even though I felt quietly ashamed of my suspicion of women with child-bearing potential, I comforted myself with a cleverly constructed application of Darwin's theory of evolution: the ideal circumstances for procreation were probably not best served by divided attention. In the way that pregnant women seem to appreciate co-expectant company, I was continuously on the lookout for peak and trough reports of sub-fertile fellow travellers, in novels and case studies, on specialised sites and blogs. My friendship with Ayane, however, was an exception to the rule; I was not entirely sure how she had managed to escape my all-consuming pregnancy-envy.

Was it because she had been there for me during one of my miscarriages, as well as its aftermath and at the subsequent 'stations of the cross'? I doubted it. It was more a case of Ayane persisting to choose for *me*. It did help that her parenting style did not breathe the air of possessive exclusivity I so resented in many of my friends. She had been determined to involve me in the birth of her daughter, five years earlier, and in the girl's every growth spurt since. There had been no room for negotiation: I was her friend and the woes of my own story were no valid excuse to miss out on hers. I did not only take it from her, Ayane's lack of patience with my occasional self-indulgence did me the world of good. On the other hand, my friend allowed me to be me, with all the complexity this entailed; she allowed me to be jealous as well as proud of this gorgeous daughter of hers.
'I don't care anymore, do you know that? Whatever happens to me and Raf and his saint Marie or to this umpteenth pregnancy: I really couldn't care less, honestly.'
'You're covering yourself. I get that.'
'Bullshit. I'm not covering myself. I mean it. I've had enough.'
'Even if you mean it, I get it.'
'Yeah, you always get everything.'
'What's that supposed to mean?' Under their sloping lids her eyes were trying to catch mine, but I kept staring into my juice refusing to play along, I was fed up with her compassion. My anger needed venting and she was there. How often had she seen me like this? How many times had she comforted and revived me, encouraged me and cheered me up? And for what? Over and over it was me who was cast in the loser's role, never her.
'That I don't even get it myself. That's what I mean.'
'That's obvious, you're living it.' There was no getting away from Ayane's logic. I realised I had once again surrendered to the loss that was soon to be

my fate. I was five weeks pregnant, I had a man who loved me dearly but whom I was pushing away. Instead I chose to lie at the bottom of my familiar pit, knees pulled up underneath me, all set to lick the fresh wounds which were about to be inflicted on me, overdosing on poor-me-ness. As she said: I was covering myself.

'I no longer make sense to myself, Ayane.'

My friend pulled me gently towards her and put her arms around me. She kissed the top of my head as I started to weep. 'What is alienating me is that I can't sincerely long for something anymore or just want something. I am a zombie.' I could feel my tears staining her purple Paul Smith top, but it was just a start, I couldn't stop. 'Shhhhh, let it go girl, that's right, let it all out.'

'Good grief, Aya.' I freed myself from her embrace but kept resting my head against her warmth; she draped an arm over my shoulder and began to stroke my neck, gently. 'Bloody hell, you really have become a professional soother, do you know that? I wonder why you still dance for a living. Any minute you're going to remind me of the pressures Raf and I have been under for years on end and how my antagonistic feelings towards Marie are but thinly veiled forms of envy of Raf's fatherhood and although unacceptable, totally understandable and so on and so on and so on.' I felt her nodding underneath me. 'O, yes and of the mere fact I'm still standing upright, I almost forgot.'

'But it's all true.'

'Aya, listen.' I took her hands in mine and looked into her eyes her eyes; it was very important she should understand this. 'This is and always was nothing more than a choice. No man, no God is doing this to us.'

'A choice', she replied dully.

'Is it not?' She ruffled through her hair and sighed, as if I were a difficult child or someone slow on the uptake. 'Come on, it stopped being that a long time ago, babe. Haven't you yourself said so yourself repeatedly, how all of this felt so double, how a force stronger than you, beyond you, seemed to push you in this direction, time and time again? But listen: forget about all that. It does not matter anymore now, does it? I have a good feeling this time round.'

'*This* time around?'

'Yes. More so than before, after the operation, with your patched-up womb and all, I am quietly confident. I am.' Her last words sounded like a question. Who was she trying to convince? I knew what she was doing and I did not want to point out that I'd heard it all before. I needed her to say these things, that was the deal. I was allowed to air my doubts and negative premonitions, it was her job to counter them. Up to this point we were both still right, neither of us had a crystal ball.

She smiled encouragingly and looked at my tight-fitting T-shirt. 'And going by those massive knockers of yours.' We both burst out laughing. It was a fact. Never before had I developed such huge, sore breasts, quite so soon. We sat together in pleasant silence for a while.

'This is not the time to kick your hope-addiction, hon. I do realise why you're so worried and why you're bracing yourself against potential setbacks. Don't you think I do that?' She smoothed her belly. Mid monologue she had got up and was pacing the room with a breadstick in her hand, waving it like a conductor, tracing elegant arcs in the air, looking not so much at me as in my direction, as if I were an audience.

'Even if I wouldn't dream of comparing my own fears with your misgivings. You can't diminish future pain by starving yourself of hope, Em. And yes, I do realise we're talking reflexes of self-protection here. I get it that you are hollowed out and that you're constantly swaying back and forth, suspended between longing and fearing and that you want to lash out at anyone who has the audacity to tell you what to do.' With this final piece of insight, she had landed cross-legged on the rug in front of me. I had to give it to her she was good. No Fleming would be able to spit out those lines unrehearsed. And yet I knew her performance was less meant to impress, than to give me credit.

'Living is persisting, Emma, wading through the shit towards the light.'

'Mmm, when you put it like that. I wish I fell for women.'

'She says now she's up the duff, the slut.'

'Aya?'

'What?'

'I miss fucking.'

'No kidding?'

'I'm serious!'

'Do you ever hear yourself talk? You've been trying for a baby for over six years; I hate to break it to you but there is more than a fleeting connection there with having sex.'

'Yes, of course. But besides that.'

'Besides what?'

'O, Shut up. Sometimes I want to be a naked body instead of a children's factory, do you understand?'

Ayane came towards me and hugged me. She pressed her pregnant tummy against mine and her modest nearly-mother-tits against my super-boobs. She was so dear to me: despite all the whimsical twists of fate we had recognised one another; there was no undoing that.

'I don't want to go home.'
'Then stay here, if you like, in Tamako's room, she'll be delighted. But you must promise to ring Raf first.'
'No way.'
'Then I will.'
'See if I care.'

I woke up with a familiar disaster-sensation, the mental hang-over reminding me of my shame, the shame of my failure. With a dysfunctional body and relationship, adversity was my karma and in the bigger cosmic picture I would be ultimately accountable.

I stayed completely still, concentrated, with my eyes closed. I felt an unmistakable pressure on my belly. Was it about to start all over again? Fortunately, I was at Ayane's already, who knew the routine and would guide me from one moment to the next. Carefully I felt my tummy; a resolute little arm was clinging to my waist. Tamako was lying on her side, with one half of her body pressed against mine. There was little difference between worry and relief. It was what I had tried to explain to Ayane the night before, how my body, almost void of feeling, had come to register and then deal with any given stimulus. To be either elated or distraught, seemed a waste of time and energy.

I stroked Tamako's smooth little crown. Straight away she opened her eyes; she was as light a sleeper as her mother.
'Auntie Em!' The girl gave me a radiant smile and squashed her face back into my neck.
'Hey, monkey.' Again, she looked up at me, eyes full of excitement, she kissed my cheek.
'Why are you here?'
'I should be asking you! When did you sneak in here, hey, hamster, go on, tell me?' I gave her playful little pinches, she giggled and fought my hand half-heartedly.
'I woke up and took some water and then I saw you, there on the other side of *Janneke moon*. She pointed out the small moon shaped light on the stool in between the two beds. *Janneke moon*, it was clear who read the bed time stories here, unless of course Ayane too had started to 'Flemify' the moon. I too was now lying on my side; I pulled her into me and caressed her warm, sleepy body. Tamako's eyes did not betray any trace of her oriental origins, in fact she did not look like either of her parents, although she indisputably had her mother's hair.
'Your mum and I stayed up chatting last night and then it had become too dark for me to go home so I thought I'd better stay for a sleep over, you know, in your room, I didn't think you'd mind.'
'No! Of course not! Were you frightened?'
'No.'

'It's quite all right, you know. There's two beds. Look.'
'Indeed. Although it seems we don't really need the other one.' Tamako smiled, she looked slightly embarrassed. 'Come here, monkey, let me squeeze you.'
'Auntie Em?'
'Yes, honey.'
'Will you tell me the story of Snegurka.'
'Again? Would you not rather hear the story of Rumpelstiltskin?' Together with Rumpelstiltskin Snegurka, the little snow girl, was Tamako's favourite. Originally this had been a story I tended to skip; as a consequence, the girl had become obsessed with it.
'No. Snegurka.'
'Ok then, are you comfy?' She nodded and pushed her body closer to mine.

'Once upon a time there was a farmer called Ivan. His wife was called Marousha. They had been together for many years, but still they did not have a child and this made them very sad. Sometimes they would look out of their window to watch the neighbouring children play, that was their only happiness. One fine winter's day, after it had been snowing all night, Ivan and Marousha watched how the children outside had fun in the snow.'
'What happened then?' Tamako's thumb disappeared into her mouth. I gently pulled it out and caressed it. 'Well, they decided to make a snow man, didn't they? In the garden in front of their small cosy cottage, they went ahead and started to gather up the snow. First they made a little body.'
'And then a little head,' Tamako continued.
'Indeed, out of which they sculpted two little holes...'
'...for the little eyes.'
'Yes. And with a small dollop of snow they made a little nose. Next a little mouth and a little chin. Then they made little hands.'
'And then little feet.'
'Yes, they did, they made little feet. Then, after a while, came a passer-by, he asked them what they were doing. We are making a snow man, Ivan said. No, a snow girl, Marousha chuckled. Ivan smiled and looked his wife in the eyes. Sorry, yes, he repeated, a snow girl. I see, may the heavens bless you, the stranger said. When he had gone, the little snow girl's lips started to move. Warm breath came from her mouth, Marousha felt it against her hand. She took a step back and looked at the snow girl. The girls gleaming eyes had turned lavender blue and her little cheeks were red.'

Tamako was sitting up and stared at my mouth as though I were the snow girl coming to life.

'But what is happening here, Ivan shouted. Is this child alive? As he spoke, the girl shook her head and with that the last snowflakes flew out of her long, blond hair. She held her pale arms up to Marousha.

'Did she call her mummy?'

'Yes, she did. *Mummy,* she said.'

'Oh, Snegurka, my very own snow girl, Marousha wept, as she held the girl. With every passing minute Snegurka grew more beautiful and more alive. In Ivan and Marousha's little cottage, where there had only ever been silence, the sound of laughter could be heard. The neighbouring children came to play with Snegurka, they taught her songs and rhymes. Snegurka was bright and learned quickly. But more than anything she loved to play in the snow with the other children. With her skilful little hands, she made magnificent snow sculptures. Ivan and Marousha thanked the heavens daily for their glorious gift. Then came spring, the sun started to warm the earth and melt the snow. The fields returned to green and the lark sang high up in the skies. Everybody was filled with joy, for the severe winter had passed; everybody except for the little snow girl, who became more withdrawn with each passing day. Marousha asked the girl what was wrong, but Snegurka shrugged her shoulders and said: nothing, I'm fine. All the snow had melted and in the fields wild flowers had sprung up and in the woods the nightingales sang their highest tunes. Everybody was happy, apart from Snegurka. She became ever sadder and started to hide in the darkest, coldest corners of the house. She was happiest playing by the water, under the shadow of the old willow tree and at night, or when heavy storms swept over the land and the wind cast its chilled breath. The corn started to ripen and the days grew longer. In the village everybody was excited, only Snegurka was not. Marousha pulled the girl on her lap, cuddled her and asked her once again what was wrong. Nothing is wrong, mummy, she said. The village children tried to cheer her up. They asked Snegurka to come along with them to the woods to pick berries or flowers, but the girl preferred to stay at home alone where she sat, wearily, in the shadow of the stone wall. But Marousha insisted: go on, go and play with the other children, darling. It will do you the world of good, you're ever so pale. At long last Snegurka gave in. Look after her well, Marousha, begged the children, Ivan and I love this girl dearly. The children nodded fiercely. And so it happened that Snegurka went along. In the woods the children started to pick berries, then flowers, which they weaved into crowns. They sang of summer and sun and of sweet ripened fruits. They became so involved in their songs that they forgot all about Snegurka, until they heard the smallest of sighs behind them. They turned around but all they saw was a small heap of melting snow. The little snow girl was nowhere to be seen. They looked everywhere and kept calling out her name. *Snegurka, where are you*? Perhaps she's gone back home, one of the children suggested. Together they ran to the village, but nobody had seen her there either. That day all the villagers went to look for Snegurka. And the next day too. But Snegurka was nowhere to be found. Ivan and Marousha were broken with sadness and for many weeks they could be heard calling: Snegurka, lovely snow girl, please come back! At times they thought they could hear her. Perhaps, when winter came, Snegurka would return.

'Mmm. Now the story of Rumpelstiltskin.'

In my head everything is simple
In my head all things have their place
In my head nothing gets mistaken
All remains unspoken
In balance, unharmed
Welcome, welcome, to my head

Raymond van het Groenewoud

'An average nuchal thickness is between one point six and three millimetres.'
'O, my God.' Raf covered his mouth with one hand but almost instantly corrected this honest reflex. Looking from me to the consultant, he did his very best to erase any alarm from his eyes. When he began to speak his voice sounded manly and in control.
'But obviously this does not necessarily mean...'
'What it means, Raf, is that the chances of a chromosomal abnormality are increased,' the consultant interrupted my husband. 'This in combination with Emma's age and blood levels gives me sufficient reason for concern, therefore, as I have suggested before, I would highly recommend further testing. CVS, which in principle can be done now, or an amniocentesis, with reduced risk of miscarriage and a more accurate picture, but which we obviously cannot carry out until later, at roughly sixteen, seventeen weeks. However, if, in the worst-case scenario, you were to decide to terminate the pregnancy at such a point, you would be considerably further along.'

He had reeled off his list, the options sounding drier that way I suppose, but there was no need; information was what I wanted from him, not a cushioned blow. What had disturbed me was the sheer logic of it all. Behind the armour of his white coat, with his omnipotent words and convincing statistics this man gave me the illusion of choice and told me to fear not, for there were no problems, only solutions to be identified. But in the end, it would be *my* body breaking the shock. Mine and my baby's.

I kept nodding, like a simpleton. It wasn't that I did not grasp the gravity of the situation, but at the same time I felt they were making such a fuss about nothing, or rather about something quite irreversible. Was I losing perspective? With the extra wall in my womb annexed and the chances to miscarry considerably reduced, the statistics seemed to have shifted and to apply to different danger zones altogether. Less than half an hour ago the ultrasound had shown us how our baby had been sucking its tiny thumb, had taken it out of his little mouth and held it up as it dealt with the hiccups. Our cautious excitement was now being crushed with new doom scenarios, theories of probability of *chromosomal* aberrations, this time. Whatever next? Anyhow, we needn't worry, a scrap of placenta or a dash of amniotic fluid would reveal the truth and nothing but the truth, so help us God. His dice would spell it out: *tough shit,* again. Or not! For what was the significance of one in two hundred? One in fifty or one in ten? If calculations were our scripture was my chance to be one of those one hundred and ninety-nine or one of those forty-nine not far greater? One of those blessed nine, rather than the fallen tenth? Where did speculating get me? All I knew was this: right now, I was eleven weeks pregnant, for years I had not dared even to speculate.

What if the test itself would become the problem and not my baby's DNA? Which risks were calculated and what amounted to Russian roulette? Why would I even consider the former unless I'd be prepared to act upon bad tidings? Which deviations of 'normal' were acceptable to me? What about Raf? Was this the same for Raf?

'Em?' Raf took my hand and looked at me intensely.
'What are you thinking?' *Stop trying so hard.*
'Are you my therapist now, or what?' I pulled my hand out of his. *Fuck. Bitch. Can't you see he's just as powerless? Don't you get that?* Raf sighed, he looked defeated.
'Sorry, *Rafke*, that was uncalled for. I did not mean it like that.' I rubbed his back. My husband was studying the tanned toes in his sandals as if they weren't his. It had been scorching hot for over two weeks now and he had been working in our garden during most of his spare time. With his elbows resting on his knees, both hands were supporting his chin.
'It's fine, love. I know.' But he didn't move; his wriggling toes needed his full attention. We'd been sitting in the waiting room for almost an hour. Any minute now, a nurse would come and talk to us and answer any remaining questions about the additional tests Mr. Plouvier had recommended. I didn't have any. I knew everything there was to know about CVS and amniocentesis; when they could be carried out and the kind of information they could and could not provide. About their respective risks of inadvertently ending the pregnancy, I had more active knowledge than most experienced nurses and possibly more than an obstetrician at the beginning of his or her career.

One in three hundred women would lose their baby as an immediate consequence of an amniocenteses, a chance of zero point three percent. Chorionic Villus Sampling or CVS, whereby a sample of cells of the placenta were removed for testing, was responsible for a miscarriage in one in every two hundred women, a chance of zero point five percent. Around week eleven, however, every pregnant woman had a natural chance of two percent of losing the pregnancy. This meant the risk of things going wrong as a consequence of CVS would increase to seven point five in three hundred; after all, how could the natural risk be distinguished from the heightened CVS risk? Seven and a half women in three hundred would effectively lose their foetus after CVS. Or were these seven and a half babies never to see the light of day? For me it was the halves more than anything, which made a mockery of probability calculation. The more I found myself clinging to percentages, the more absurd and irrelevant they became. In fact, I had already thrown in the towel as far as further testing was concerned: I wanted to surrender to this endearing little hitchhiker I'd seen on the screen earlier that day. At long last I was ready to believe that it was possible. I was ready to believe that my body could do it, that I could do it. There I was, ready to believe in the promise of life and embrace it. But there was one problem: it wasn't just mine to embrace.

'What if I feel differently now, then what? Or am I obliged to stick with something I claimed years ago, in a hypothetical context? People change, Raf, and what they want and are able to deal with changes with them.' It was after nine but our terrace was still bathed in an oppressive heat. After we had returned from the hospital we agreed to go for an Italian around the corner from where we lived. We must have both felt it would better to have this talk on neutral ground. But the actual precarious dialogue had not erupted until we were back home, having a night cap in the garden. Raf took a greedy gulp from his Hoegaarden. I could have murdered a cool pint, but instead I frugally sipped from my tonic water.
'Don't you get that this feels so very different for me now?'
'And don't *you* get that you can't simply change your mind about decisions of this weight? Have you any idea what you are asking of me here, Emma? You're hardly urging me to consider a second car or a leather sofa instead of a fabric one, are you?' I had fished a slice of lemon out of my glass and was gnawing at its rind. 'I am aware of that.'
'Besides it is not the first time we've discussed these issues, is it? Hypothetically, of course, how else? But certainly not years ago, this is

hardly your first pregnancy.' That he shouldn't have said, not like that anyway. 'Thanks a lot, Raf.' I got up and walked away, into the living room. I was not really offended but I felt intimidated by his logic. Was everything rhetoric? Would the more articulate one of us win the argument in the end? He followed me, beer glass in hand.

'Please, Emma, don't get all oversensitive now. Don't you think this is traumatic for me?'

'But it shouldn't be, should it? After all this time, I'm pregnant, I finally remain pregnant but we seem determined to scrutinise this baby, to reassure ourselves it's ok. Whereas instead we could be enjoying the process and hope for the best with our fingers crossed. How do you think people did this in the olden days?'

'In the olden days? That's a good one! I hate to be the one to spoil your fantasies about times gone by, honey, but in those golden olden days of yours, short of the moral dilemmas brought on by all this testing, you would not even have been pregnant in the first place.' I did not say anything. Raf was trying to catch my eyes. 'Wouldn't you say? Listen to me, Emma, an amnio does not just give clarity about Downs, you know.'

'I know that.'

'If the picture has changed for you and you were to be able to accept a child with Downs, let's have that discussion when there is certainty. Who knows, I might feel different myself at that point.

'Then why testing, Raf? Isn't that insane, running the risk of a miscarriage when all the while the baby might not be…shit, I can't even say it.' He sat down beside me and took me in his arms. '*Emmetje*, my darling, because there might be defects we would *not* be able to live with and because it appears that risk is relatively high, that's why. Also, because, if the baby were indeed to have Downs and I would be able to come round to that, it still would be far better to have the time to get used to that.'

Raf stroked my belly and carefully started to kiss me. It all sounded so reasonable coming from him. How I longed to hand everything over. I suddenly wanted to have sex; I kissed him back, caressed his tongue with mine.

'Raf?'

'Yes?'

'What if I have another miscarriage?' Raf unbuttoned my blouse, he was suddenly in a hurry as he stroked my huge breasts. 'There is very little chance at that, darling, you know that. You're almost twelve weeks along, it is obvious the operation was a success. Now all the risks that remain are the utterly minimal ones every woman runs when undergoing an amniocentesis: zero point three percent. I can understand that with all that you've been through, even that is scary. But just try to have a little faith, all right?' There was nothing I wanted more and with enormous relief I started to undo my husband's fly.

The day before the amniocenteses Ayane's water broke. It somehow gave me a strange feeling of connection, all the more because we would end up in the same hospital. She rang me before she had even told Luc and sounded astonishingly serene.
'With a bit of luck, we'll end up shuffling through the corridors arm in arm, Em, in our battered bath robes.' I smiled. 'I will need to stay horizontal, you know, after the amnio.'
'Yes, of course, I forgot about that. Well, they'll have to wheel me and the baby to you then.'
How I envied her unwavering trust in positive outcomes. Unlike me, Ayane did not contemplate versions of events in which things went wrong or worse, hold the superstitious belief that failing to consider negative scenarios, would end up bringing them about. I liked it that she acted normally and didn't even consider so called sparing my feelings. She did not comment on the amniocentesis either, what would be would be. I myself was a bag of nerves, exhausted from swaying back and forth in my own head. I still wasn't convinced our decision was the right one. My relief about Raf taking charge had been short lived.
'Emma?'
'Yes?'
'Good luck, my love.'
'Thanks, you too.'
'Aishiteru.'
'Me too.'

Less than twenty-four hours later Ayane was indeed wheeled to my room. I knew nothing yet of the baby boy she had left in Luc's care on the maternity ward. I myself had lost my healthy daughter one hour after the amniocentesis.

And so it came to be that, on the evening of our respective deliveries, my best friend once again sat by my bedside, albeit slightly less composed than she normally was.

'*Emmetje*, o my darling girl.' As soon as she saw me the tears started to roll down her face as she was searching for my hand under the sheets. She looked absolutely shattered. A while ago one of the nurses had offered me a tranquiliser, I wanted to comfort my friend but I literally lacked the strength. 'Aya.' My tongue felt like a dried-out sponge. Ayane squeezed my hand hard and started to cry again, small, delicate sobs. I thought of her face, as if she wasn't there, nor I, how sweet it looked in all its distress, her eyes even more flat now, sunken and wet.

'I want to come closer but I can't, the operation you see, I had an emergency Caesarean last night, Emma.'

'O. Are you... did you...is everything all right?'

'Shush, later.' Her hand had let go of mine, with the sleeve of her bath robe she rubbed her eyes. Was there more than my own curse? Was that why she couldn't stop crying? Had there been complications with her labour? She was sobbing even more uncontrollably now. I managed to bend slightly and smoothed her hair with my fingertips.

'Ayane?'

'A son, Takuya, shhhh. O Emma, it's not fair.' I sank back into the pillows.

The feeling came pure and with it solace, the balm of relief. This was what would sustain me: what I felt was undiluted relief about the healthy birth of my friend's baby boy. By no means euphoria, but not resentment either. *Takuya.* In my head I tried out his name.

There could never been absolute proof that the amniocentesis had been the cause of my fifth miscarriage. The surgeon who had reconstructed my uterus was convinced it had been. The consultants at the hospital where I had had the procedure believed the likelihood minimal and backed up their theories with my own abominable reproductive history.

With this the chance-dance had begun again. I had suspected that, if fate were to strike again, I would not care less about the ins and outs, the actual details. The opposite was true: more than ever I wanted to *know* and *understand*. I was obsessively interested in every tiny detail related to my loss and I would do everything needed to find out which of the two hypotheses was the more likely. Years later my shrink would decode this urge as the onset of closure.

Part 2

'I am so very proud of you, girl!' Raf was waiting in the wings with a big bunch of flowers. He was about to grab hold of me but was beaten to it by Tweedle Dee and Tweedle Dum, who were pulling on either side of my skirt in an attempt to drag me back onto the stage for a third time, it was becoming a bit embarrassing. I offered a coy little bow and again waved to the audience; I stuck up my thumb to the line of actors who were showing off next to me on the stage.

'Well done, guys, really. There will be a well-deserved Oscar party next week!'

'Yes!' Rabbit brushed his hand through his purple hair, pulled back his punky spikes and pumped the air. 'And the winner is...Nivens McTwisp!' The curtain closed and from all corners mums came running towards their child actors with emergency drinks, tissues and carrier bags with 'civilian' clothing. The noise was deafening. 'Miss, can we do *Narnia* next year?' The frail, freckled girl in the crooked hat looked straight at me, pleading; the artificial hair that was sticking out at the sides was almost the same colour as her own. 'Marieke, please! Can we recover from *Alice* first?' I pulled her to me and kissed her rosy cheek.

Less than a year ago I had started my own children's theatre. As a freelance I was linked up with a number of local primary schools. Initially I had done a few taster workshops in the hope of generating interest amongst pupils and staff in more long-term projects which would eventually lead to a performance. For a small fee Joris Durrant, the head master of one of these schools, had offered me the use of an impressive rehearsal space on Wednesday and Saturday afternoons. I was free to dress it as I pleased. As well as that, there was the option to rent the sports hall for performances. It came with a real stage, dressing rooms and light and sound equipment. When that time came, he had added, he'd be more than happy to help me out; the school was in need of a fresh creative breeze.

I estimated Joris to be a few years younger than myself. He was a charismatic man with intense blue eyes and a tremendous sense of humour, in fact he looked a bit like Ralph Fiennes. I was looking forward to working with him.

From the start the enterprise had been a huge success, it was clear we had identified a gap in the market. Soon there was no more need for me to take on work as an actor. I was getting so much work that Raf offered to turn our double garage into a work space for me, in that way I would be able to operate more independently.

The idea came from Luc, Ayane's husband.
About a month after Takuya's birth, I was to spend a girl's night at my friend's while her husband was at work. By eight thirty, however, Luc was back home; the show had been cancelled, one of the dancers had had a fall and broken his wrist.
'Ok, honey, I'm off.' I grabbed my pull-over from the back of the sofa.
'Why? Because of *him*?' Ayane started to top up my glass in protest. 'Don't mind me girls, I'm about to have a long soak and then I ...' A penetrating wail erupted from the baby's room.
'... I am going to feed my son and only *then* shall I have a bath, after which time I'll probably go on the internet for a bit and then I may well join you girls for a drink', Ayane finished his sentence.
'Do you hear that, Emma? Ever wondered who's wearing the pants in this house?' I was fond of Luc; he was an uncomplicated, decent guy and a wonderful, hands-on father. He was one of the few men I knew who could multitask like a woman. But then I guess I was in the habit of projecting onto other people's relationships all that was missing in my own; lately that was an awful lot. There was a time I had felt guilty about my persistent nagging about Raf's shortcomings. Now my conscience was no longer bothering me; every relatively peaceful day with him felt like a concession. In my head nothing was peaceful, but I lacked the courage and the energy to talk to him. What was the point?

The baby's crying grew more urgent. 'Jesus, fierce little Jap.' In pretend exasperation Raf fled to the kitchen where he busied himself with bottles and milk. The entire house was tastefully open plan. 'Fierce little Flem, you mean.' Ayane stretched her long ballerina neck. 'He's a fierce little Flap, my godson,' I settled the score.
'Cheers to the Flap,' Ayane raised her glass and toasted in her best Flemish.
Luc pressed the rubber teat of the bottle into the back of his hand and threw a tea towel over his shoulder, nonchalant gestures of habit, worlds away from mine. About to release his yelping cub, he walked behind the sofa and planted a kiss on his wife's head. 'No peace with all these oriental tyrants under one roof.' Ayane craned her neck and presented her pursed lips, eyes closed. The entire domestic scene gave me a pang. It wasn't jealousy or

envy even, what I felt had moved beyond that. I wanted to *be* them, or anyone else for that matter, whose life ran according to some plan, or perhaps just ran. But what did I really know of Luc and Ayane at night, zonked and sleep deprived, the artist and her artisan, the elusive beauty and her earthy Fleming?

'Don't lose any more weight, Em. You're almost too thin.'

'Why do you think I'm snacking on these wine-calories?' My friend kept staring at me without cracking a smile; she was not going to be deterred from her caring role.

'Things all right between you and Raf?'

'O, let me see, Raf and me? We're like two turtle doves, really.' I studied an olive before putting it into my mouth.

'Mmm, can't be easy.'

'Not easy? Bit of an understatement.' I sighed. 'Ayane?'

'What?'

'I'd like to propose something.'

'O dear. Go on then, fire away.'

'I'd like to try, as much as possible at least, to spare you my restlessness, my angst. I've got my professional lady now, haven't I? When I'm with you I want to have fun and get drunk and watch stupid films, and pamper my godson. What do you say?'

'Don't be like this, Emma. I don't deserve it.'

I looked straight at her, I meant it. I felt I owed her a different me. 'That's right, you don't deserve this. You don't deserve my constant upset. You're forever the strong one, you never complain, I'm sure your own life isn't always 'Little house on the prairie', is it? But I'm always the moaner.' Ayane rolled her eyes. 'I'm not jealous or anything, or angry, it's just…I'm so fed up with the sound of my own whining voice and I want to be able to tell you that. I want you to help me tap into this other me when we're together, don't you see?'

Ayane bit her thumb nail. Was this hard for her?

'Of course I do. But now I get the feeling you are trying to exclude me, Em and that you want us to start up some fake sharing platform, sunny side up, happy clappy and all that shit.' She took a firm swig of her wine and planted her glass on the coffee table, annoyed. I poured us more wine. I was not sure what exactly I expected from her in this new role, but somehow it felt vital for the preservation of our friendship. 'Aya, there is not just the Raf-and-Em-dialogue which is in need of rewriting, our script has changed too.'

'O my God, I hear this shrink woman talking now, sorry, honey, it gives me the creeps.'

'Yes! Of course, you hear my therapist talking through me, rather obvious, no? If she made no connection, no difference to my reality and my way of dealing with stuff, what good would it do? She's supposed to give me insight, strategies to deal with things, she's supposed to help me tell the wood from the trees, deal with this pile of shit I call my life.'

'Your life isn't a pile of shit, Emma. You have not brought any of this on to yourself.'

'Do you really think I don't know that? But do you think it helps me feel better? Do you reckon it's enough for someone to provide me with a number of crass, intellectual insights, for me to feel less shit? To *feel* less? Don't you think I had those clever insights already?'

'Am I interrupting anything?'

'No, Luc, not at all. Here, grab a glass.' This was odd. I had only just resigned from my victim role and already I felt less feeble. Ayane was sitting on the rug, slightly slumped, she seemed to be sulking. Did she feel rejected? Reprimanded? Was she about to step into my former role? Was it that simple? Would there always be the need for a perpetrator and a victim?

'Aya?'

'Sorry? What?'

'It's ok for Luc to join us, right?' My friend looked startled.

'Yes, of course it is, what kind of a question is that?' Luc felt the tension in the air; he looked from me to his wife.

'I was just telling Ayane that I want to stop off-loading so much on to her, that I realise it has begun to define the dynamics of our friendship and I have started to feel awkward about it lately and guilty. Now she thinks I'm beginning to sound like my shrink.'

'Wow. I thought you were just having a few drinks. A bit heavy, no?'

Ayane and I looked at each other and burst into laughter.

'Little house on the prairie,' she said in a toneless voice. 'Cow.' I started to hum the theme tune. 'How many crates have you had?'

It had turned into a magical evening. When Raf came to pick me up and joined us for a quick drink, we were in full flow planning my children's theatre. It had started with Luc's light-hearted, yet brave remark that a life without kids in it did not seem an option for me. He proclaimed I had this gift, this talent for kids, that I 'got' them. I owed it to myself, he said, to keep on drawing from that well, to keep on feeding this hunger to play and work and grow alongside young people. It had nurtured my battered soul. In the early hours Raf had ceremoniously drafted a plan of action which the four of us had to sign. The small print stipulated that Luc, who gave birth to this initiative, was to hold the patent. Finally, the plan was toasted once again and the couch was pulled out; Ayane insisted that Raf and I should stay the night.

At half past two that morning I found myself in the rocking chair in the nursery holding Takuya in my arms. I told him all about my plan: one day he'd be Peter Pan in his godmother's play.
Sleep tight, little Pete, auntie Emma's special treat.

When I came back from my therapist one day, the session I was replaying in my head reminded me of an inferior episode of *In Treatment*; the acting unconvincing, the script uninspired. No bold confessions of festering secrets, their drives unearthed with seeming ease by a judicious shrink. What was lacking was the force of a truth exposed. We did not even try to avoid the clichés.

'Have you any idea where this anger stems from?' My God, did she really need to ask?

'What? Here and now or way back?'

'How do you mean, Emma?'

'Well,' I knew I sounded pedantic. 'What I said: is the question *when did my frustration with Raf begin* or *what made me such a live wire to start with*? That's what I mean.'

I was getting worked up. This too I recognised from parodies of therapies: I was acting the archetypal defiant client. What else could I do? Any minute now she would insinuate that I was obstructing the procedure, although she'd make it sound like a warm invitation to trust the process.

But she didn't say anything, which was just as predictable, of course. As was my behaviour: her mere reference to my anger had been all it took to ruffle my feathers.

How exactly was this infantile war of words going to help me?

'I'm dissatisfied, yes, I have been for years.' She nodded. Her face did not betray anything, no surprise, no empathy, nothing. 'Can you remember when this started?'

'I know where you're heading, it's my unfulfilled desire for a child grieving me. I figured that one out myself.'

'I'm not heading anywhere, Emma.' Her hands were resting in her lap, one in the other, every now and then this tight hermetic grip would slightly open up. 'I have no clearly defined destination. I think one could say that I'm going wherever you wish to take me, not the other way round. But I feel it could be useful if we were to identify your distress and find out if you feel more betrayed by your husband than by your body.' I looked at her in shock and the remainder of our session I used to scrutinise her choice of words, fighting any possible breakthrough.

Later that night I rang Ayane to give her a breakdown of the session. This had become my way of involving my friend, without burdening her too much.

'Is that how she said it?'
'Word for word.'
'Then I think the woman has integrity. I agree, it's about time you answer that question.'

Even though Ayane was my harshest critic, she remained my best buddy and the main provider of distraction. We would talk less and less about my heartache and somehow that had injected a girly frivolousness into our bond. Ayane was very serious about the duties of a godmother and insisted I should spend regular time with Takuya. At first, I had accused her of charity. Shortly after Takuya was born, Raf and I had been invited to dinner. When we sat down for aperitif, Luc walked in with an ice bucket. He put on a grave face as he took out a dripping bottle of Veuve Clicquot, Ayane suddenly looked uncomfortable. For one scary moment I thought they would have the bad taste to toast the healthy arrival of their baby boy. Raising the bottle up in the air Luc looked directly at me, Ayane started nodding. 'Emma, we...we wanted to ask you something tonight.' Good grief. What was going on? The happy couple exchanged a glance. 'We were wondering if you would do us the honour of becoming Takuya's godmother,' Luc said, with a thin smile.

Raf was the first to give an answer, something I would reproach him about later, that he had influenced my decision, that he did not have the right.

'Wow, Em', he said, radiant smile. I was staring into space, stiffly holding out my hand full of pistachios. I looked at Luc, then at Ayane, baffled, stuck. 'O,' I said.

'Well? What are your thoughts?' She knew damn well what my thoughts were. Saint Aya the compassionate, knew all about my black energy, my nasty colliding, forever comparing, bloody thoughts. But she would exorcise them, wouldn't she? If anyone could bend them, align them and feng-shui them, those spiteful thoughts of envy and resentment, it would be her. She was the wise one, the intuitive and the free one. Was that because she was Japanese or Ayane? Or because she had had a baby? She had wanted one and got it. I had never felt more owed, so much for my shrink. 'O, goodness, me, there's a surprise,' I faked. The cork popped and the flutes were filled and clinked against one another. There was a brief silence and then the conversation just meandered on as before. Gossip about the opera, the planned redundancies that were the result of corporate restructuring, the talk of the day.

Ayane had decamped to the kitchen to start on the dinner. I followed her, hanging on to my champagne glass.

'Aya?'

'O, lovie, lovie, thank you, this will be the best thing, no?' I fell into her arms and started to cry. My confusion was real. As was my annoyance. 'This is my consolation prize, isn't it?' I asked her through my tears.

Only once would I ever see her as angry as this. Ayane stamped her feet, furious, Rumpelstiltskin, whose name I had guessed, whose baby I now would get. 'Fuck! Fuck! I knew it! I knew you would think that and that is so bloody unfair, Emma and so bloody untrue! If you had been standing here in front of me today, with that delightful belly of yours, with that little girl of yours in it, God forbid, I swear, I would still have, we would still have, that was the deal for God's sake, Luc and I had always planned to...you stupid woman, fuck!'

Ayane tore off her apron with one hand, flung it to the floor, together with the little oil brush she was holding in the other hand and raged up the stairs. From the living room the soft sound of laughter against the background of Miles Davis's 'Sketches of Spain'.

The plan, predetermined or not, worked. Takuya and I developed invincible alliance. My silly faces would elicit the most excited laughter, my hands were the most skilful at soothing nasty belly cramps and it was in my direction Takuya's first staggering and unsteady steps would lead.

'Of course it doesn't have to be.'

'What?'

'Australia. It doesn't have to be Australia, I said.'

'No?' I looked up from my work.

'You have always wanted to go to Chile, right?'

'Yes, that's true. I suppose that's an option.' I continued to tap the keyboard. I wasn't really listening. Raf was scanning travel sites on his laptop, I was editing my latest script on mine. Lately this was the nearest we got to 'together-time': ping-ponging interjections back and forth over our respective screens. Random ideas, bits of thought, little jokes, anything was game as long as it remained light and airy and did not approach this all-encompassing sadness of mine, which is how Raf had referred to my grieving process during our last big fight.

Six weeks after the loss of our baby, I received a letter from the hospital with the official declaration that *there was no evidence of any causal connection between the early termination of the pregnancy and the amniocentesis, and that the probability of there being any such a connection was no more than 0.3%.* Before I left the hospital, I had insisted on a conversation with someone from the ombud service. Ten days later, a meeting was arranged for Raf and me with the consultants concerned as well as with someone from the medical team who had been present. They even gave us the option of a video screening of the fateful procedure during the meeting. The sense of tact and timing of those people knew no limits – I had of course declined the offer. Raf had hardly said a single word during the conversation, in the course of which, for form's sake, the medics reeled off their well-rehearsed *no-blame-can-be-attached-to-us* refrain for the umpteenth time. So as not to send me home again empty-handed, the mediating ombudsman assured us that he would personally follow up on the case and provide us with a final written report.

The letter ended with the proviso that by now I knew by heart, where the patient was advised to be aware of the possible risks of an amniotic fluid puncture as a result of which neither the hospital nor the doctor involved could be made responsible for any eventual complications that might occur. Attached was a copy of the statement and beneath it my own unmistakable, illegible signature.

'Cowardly bastards.'

'Well, what did you expect, love?' Raf stood behind me, holding firmly onto my shoulders while he read along. I'd wanted to push his hands off, so I could read the letter first.

'They can't prove that, just as Doctor Verdonck is never going to admit his operation wasn't a success for the simple reason no one knows that.' I didn't want to hear what he had to say. I couldn't afford to. But I also knew that I wouldn't be able to control myself much longer. 'Can't you even begin to understand my reaction, Raf?'

'Course, course I can.' I paced up and down between the settee and the table, waving the letter in my hand. I stopped and looked at Raf, which wasn't easy. 'Can't you get it into your thick skull that I can't get by without some explanation or other? I'm not Job, for god's sake, who at every new disaster steels himself for the next one!'

'Emma! This isn't some sort of personal battle. This is simply *force majeure* and huge, heart-breaking bad luck!'

I was capable of concocting a snide reply with each of those words: bad luck, battle, force majeure. He had no right to use them, his unctuous voice desecrated their true meaning. He was the cowardly bastard, not the administrative employee at the hospital who had copied my declaration and typed this letter and put it in the out-tray. 'Not some sort of personal battle, Ralf? Not some sort of personal loss?'

'I didn't say that.'

'Not, you didn't have to,' I muttered. I sat down at the table and held the letter in front of me. I had to read it once more – perhaps I had missed something. 'What did you say?'

'Nothing.'

'What did you say, Emma, because I'm ready for it. In fact, I've been waiting for it.'

'For what?'

Raf shook his head and lumbered out of the living-room. It was what he did when a storm was brewing, as if our room was a stage and he went off into the wings to consult his script. I followed him into the kitchen. 'Come on, then, waiting for what?' I struck a defiant pose in front of him, arms folded, almost revelling in the menacing turn things had taken.

'For your accusation, Emma. Don't you know it's something I'm aware of all the time? Or do you really think you're able to disguise it? Every moment of the day – in your eyes and your evasive gestures and your sighs I sense it – the accusation you hardly manage to suppress.'

His face was right next to mine – I could smell coffee and cigarettes. He had taken up smoking again on our judgment day; it no longer mattered.

'How dare you?'

'How I dare? I'll tell you how I dare – we had an agreement, Emma. We were going to try one more time and if it didn't work, we would try to pick up the pieces, pull our life together back to where we'd left it almost ten years ago – and try to help each other. And then, miracle of miracles, you got pregnant and at long last everything looked fine and we were through the worst bit, and then...'

'And then what, Raf?' I screamed into his face. 'Tell me, I'd love to know, then what? And then you absolutely had to go overboard and follow that bloody doctoral fraternity and their obsession with testing and raking in the shekels, despite the risks! Have you any idea how much money they pull in from doing those sorts of routine checks? Have you never suspected that might have something to do with their overreaction?'

'Oh my God Emma, you're such a bloody hypocrite! You've insisted on tests and treatments for years on end – you couldn't get enough of them! Because money was never to be an issue; you steamed right ahead, dragging me in your trail as a necessary evil, as your very own fertilising machine. As long as it resulted in a baby, no needle prick was too much, no operation ever too scary or expensive. When at long last, I dared to refer to this fertility circus as a money grabbing business, you cursed me and had the audacity to call me a traitor, remember? Or have you erased that memory too, along with that of all those other miscarriages *not* caused by a puncture? 'Bastard.' I spat it out, under my breath, hardly audible. 'What was that? What did you say? Bloody hell, woman, you know full well I did not decide on this procedure on my own, nor on a whim, that the consultant had very strong indications to suggest...' 'To suggest what, Raf? Strong indications of what? Bullshit! She was perfectly healthy! Perfect, she was! And oh yes, well done mate, I thought the penny would never drop: indeed, it was on my own that I raced ahead, too right, with needles stuck in *my* body, hands poking and pulling at *me* for years on end, it was *my* solitary battle, you'd long had enough, Raf, for you there was not really any need, was there, you *had* your daughter, didn't you? And then, when it finally started to look as though it might happen, after all that, after all the wretched mess, the tide was turning and your new child became almost tangible and I was dying to reason with you and I wanted to reclaim my own body, but you stopped me. Call me twisted, Raf, but I knew it, I knew it, I had a premonition, deep down, that things would go wrong.' 'Bravo! Some fortune teller you are! It's gone wrong every single bloody time! Chances are that without the puncture you would have lost the pregnancy again anyhow, but no, that wouldn't do, would it? That wouldn't suit you, that's not quite the scenario you wish to cling to, is it?' 'My God: the pregnancy. You still can't utter the words, can you? You lost your *daughter*, but then again, you already had one, right? I don't know how I could have been so stupid. Why have I never seen this before? You are the prosecutor here. In all those long, suffering years of yours, with your so called noble, empathic sighs and honourable silences, it was you who condemned me. My obsession with becoming pregnant, the expensive drugs and treatments, my job resignation, my need for compassion, my emotional unavailability, my all-consuming urge to have, no, to *steal* your child, you've had it up to here, you're fed up!' 'Spot on, my clever wife! But by all means, let's not forget this: that all-encompassing sadness of yours, the suffocating blanket of your endless self-pity!

Raf, true to form, stormed out of the house.

I sat on the sofa and studied my trembling hands. A familiar wave of panic engulfed me; I felt as if I was spilling over into my surroundings, I became one with the cushions and the rug. There I was: numb, objectified, matter to matter.

I got up and walked into the living room. The letter was lying on the floor. I bent down and picked it up, my head felt light. Stealthily I read a few words: *termination of the pregnancy… no more than 0.3%.* Words without meaning, their context escaped me. In an impulse I ripped up the letter and scattered the pieces around me. 'Bastards, fucking bastards! Wretched, bloody cowards!'

I sat down at the table; I hoped a plan would unfold. But my head failed me, it was far too heavy. I lowered it into my arms and tried to breathe, in and out. Something was weighing on my chest, pressing, obstructing the flow of my breathing.

The sobbing took off gently, almost beyond my control. But with every gulp it grew less and less contained. The more I lashed out, the more I seemed to unleash. It felt not unlike heaving and throwing up. Gushes of bother, like bile, came pouring out. Gasps of breath, carrying sorrow and loathing and self-pity, staggered from peak to peak, wailing, collapsing waves of pained breath. In the end my lament settled into a soft, comfortable humming, like the sound of a well-oiled motor with regular, yawning intermezzos. At last my oddly satisfying outburst had fizzled out in the vague anticipation of the next day: my meeting with Joris, the prospect of swollen eyelids with no make-up to be rescued. And there it was again, the voice of reason. Who gave the signal? How long was an outpouring of grief to last? How long a relationship? The dilemma which had been ruling most of my adult life. How long was I to persist, to keep on trying against the odds? When was I to recognize when enough was enough? It was vital for me to vent my anger, but in the aftermath, I was left hankering for peace. Nothing would ever stop me wanting, but the weight of the wanting itself.

I became aware of the silence around me. I got up and frantically began to pick up the bits of scattered paper. I put them on the table and started to puzzle them back together; here was a *rewind* I could achieve. I walked over to the chest of drawers, took out the sellotape, sat down and concentrated on the task at hand, it was a soothing little job. Bit by bit the letter came back to life, as a restored version of itself. *'...the pregnancy and the amniocentesis, and that the probability.'* Pregnancy, there it was, in black and white, it was true. It really had happened.

The following morning, I had a meeting with Joris Durrant. Raf hadn't come home that night, his mobile phone was lying on the bedside table. I had slept two hours at the most and it showed. I looked and felt absolutely shattered.

'Emma, good morning, come in. How are you?' Joris kissed my cheek. His was smooth and cool.

He smelt nice, a mixture of expensive aftershave and sports gear.

'O, ça va.' I threw my bag on one of the two chairs in front of his desk. The un-alluring seat for worried parents, indignant about their child's behaviour or the far too lenient school policies.

I pointed at the percolating coffee maker in the corner. 'Would it be alright for me to grab a coffee?' Joris shut the door and looked at me. 'Here, sit down, let me do that.' He poured me a cup and put it down in front of me on the desk. Black, he remembered. I had dreamt of him a few days before, steamy flashes of the film adaptation of 'The End of the Affair', which I had been to see with Ayane. I, of course, collided with the Juliane Moore-character, Joris and Fiennes had blurred into one. The rest of the week I had tried to recreate the dream. Joris put my bag on the floor and sat down beside me. He put his hand on my arm.

'You ok, Emma?'

'A bit tired, that's all. I think I'm coming down with something.'

'I can tell, you don't look yourself. Go back to bed, girl, we can meet some other time, can't we?' The word 'bed' gave me an electric shock. I was impossible. Joris kept looking at me as he raised his eyebrows. Fiennes as 'Hamlet'. At that point my mobile went off.

Raf told me he'd been at a friend's and was about to set off back home. I think I was supposed to read remorse into that. I said that I couldn't care less, I wasn't at the house anyway. When I walked through the school gates I knew exactly what to do. I'd go to Ayane's and probably stay the night, again. It was like playing chess, keeping a relationship spinning; every move of the other determined one's own follow up strategy and vice versa. I called my friend. By all means I was welcome, she sounded chuffed.

'Sorry, honey, I look crap.' Ayane brushed my cheek with her lips. Her faded, baggy T-shirt was covered in stains. With it she wore a shapeless pair of shorts that covered her legs almost up to her delicate little knees, most likely a pair of Luc's cast offs. In her arms Takuya screamed his little head off.

'See if I care.' I kissed her.

'*Takske*! God, how he has grown!' I held my arms out.

'Don't call him that.' Ayane was too tired to genuinely object to her son's nickname and practically threw him into my arms. He was screeching at the top of his voice. 'O, little teddy of mine, what's the matter? Hey? Come on, sweetheart, you can tell your auntie Em.' Lo and behold the boy stopped crying and stared at me with huge, wet eyes.

'Look, Aya, quick, he's smiling!'

'Yeah, yeah, whatever. You're welcome to him. Honestly, Em, I'm truly and totally fed up with the brat.' She slowly punctuated each syllable. 'I've had my third consecutive sleepless night and I'm climbing the walls, I'm not kidding you.'

'O, teddykins, what's mummy saying, hey? Hello, Bibsee, hello! Where's your godmummy, hey? What's going on, my naughty little ratbag?'

'Tea?'

'Yes, please.'

'Green?'

'Perfect.'

Ayane shuffled into the kitchen and started to bang the doors of the designer cupboards. I followed her in, Takuya on one arm; he took great delight in his mother's manic bashings.

'Shit.'

'What?'

'None left. There's never anything in this wretched place unless I get it myself. Himself is off squashing.'

'Water's fine too.'

'Sorry, none left in the tap. Joke!' she shouted too loud, after which she burst into hysteric laughter. 'Aya, is everything all right?'

'Hec no! O, Emma, I feel so...flap.'

'So what?'

'Flap.' She flapped her arms about in the air.'

'How do you mean?'

'Never mind, I have no words. I feel like jumping out of my own skin, spraying graffiti on the neighbour's walls, directing the traffic, massaging fat men, anything other than being glued to the walls of this wretched, perfect hole!'

'Wow.'

'What?'

'Finally.'

'Emmetje! Forgive me my narcissism. Of course, you've come to see me about your own troubles, sorry.'

'Pfff. What's new about that?'

'Nonsense. Things are looking up lately, aren't they? With all those big plans of yours?'

I shrugged my shoulders. 'Can we talk about something else?' I sat down in the rocking chair with my godson, careful not to make any sudden move, his little shrimpy claw was tightly curled around my index finger.

'Sure, honey, sure. Look at the little monster.' She looked down upon her son, endeared, who had fallen asleep in my arms. I could tell she was relieved about my holding back and who could blame her? How long could we go on ruminating on my woes?

'Can I take a really quick shower, Em?' She sounded at the height of helplessness, nothing mattered anymore, she might as well end it.

'Of course. Why do you ask?'

'You ok here, with *Takske*?'

'What does it look like?' She hesitated for a moment, at the door and turned back. All at once she seemed to wake up from her lethargy. 'Emma!'

'What?'

'I have a plan!' she shouted ecstatically. I groaned. 'O, no, please, not a plan.'

'No, really, hear me out.' She knelt down on the floor beside me and grabbed the arm of the chair to stop it rocking. Her voice still sounded desperate, as though the idea that I might turn down her proposition was too awful to contemplate.

'Luc's not working tonight, he can stay with the kids. We could get dolled up and hit the town, what do you say? Yes? Smashing plan, or what?'

'Ooo,' I sighed. 'Do I have to act all excited now as well? Fine, yes, whatever. Didn't bring anything to wear mind you, was not exactly in that kind of mood.' Her eyes were still fixed on me, her face a mixture of hope and uncertainty. 'So? Just borrow something of mine? What about the red *Miu Miu* fuck-me dress, hey? How long have you been dying to get your mits on that? Go on, confess.'

'Get into your shower, Aya. We'll see about that later.'

'Hurray! I have a date!' She pulled her scruffy T-shirt over her head, wiggled her mini-tits like a fully-qualified pole dancer and headed for the bath-room.

'I really don't feel like going on holiday with him for the moment, honestly.' I took a sip from my mojito. 'Not too much rum in this, is there?'

'Not a generous portion, not really, no.' Aya looked around, excitedly, like a teenager clubbing for the first time. 'But he doesn't mean this instant, does he? I mean, a holiday needs planning and booking and what have you. You can't go until the summer anyway, with your production.'

'It didn't literally mean *at this moment*, it's just, any mention of it feels too soon after...'

'After all that shit.'

'Err yes, you could say that. Gosh, you have such a way with words.'

'Sorry.'

'No, not at all, shit covers it just fine.'

'Em?'

'Mmm?'

'I don't want to interfere or anything but why don't you come to Sardinia with us this summer? The house we're renting is enormous. I'd really love to have you there, so would the kids, I know, and Luc too I think, I know.'

'Did you discuss it with him?'

'A bit.'

'A bit?'

'Just tested the water, you know.'

'And?'

'Yes, he seems to like the idea. Gives him the option to have some bloke time with Raf, we two could spend some time together too, we could take it in turns for meals and for the kids and that, very practical. I can only see advantages.'

'Really? We all know that going on holiday with friends can be incredibly testing.'

'You need to make clear arrangements, that's key. I admit it's a bit of a gamble, but come on, Emma, we've survived worse than a few holiday irritations, haven't we? And even if they do pop up, we're not petty people, are we? But I think it is much more likely everything will run smoothly and we will all have the holiday of a lifetime.'

'I don't know. I'm not sure it's Raf's thing, you see. But it's a very kind offer, thank you.'

'Just think about it, ok? Discuss it with Raf.' I gave her a querulous look.

'Well, when you're back on speaking terms, I mean.' Then she tactfully changed the subject.

'You look stunningly hot in that dress, do you know that?' She stroked my calf with her high heeled foot. 'Any plans tonight, gorgeous?' I closed my eyes and kissed the air.

'God, I can hardly remember it all, flirting, seducing, sex, the whole bloody Kama Sutra.'

'Are you serious? You sound rather angry.'

'Do you know I've been sleeping in Takuya's room for weeks now, rather than with Luc? He's an absolute pain lately.'

'Who? Tak or Luc?'

'Both.'

'Sorry, I had no idea.'

'No. Of course you haven't. In your eyes everything that springs from the cord promotes bliss.

'Luc is trying his hardest, isn't he?'

'That's just it: my man is trying his hardest.'

'I don't get it.'

'I know you don't.'

'But you reveal so little, Ayane. You always expect me to bare my soul but you yourself...'

Ayane stared into her glass. Was she finally toying with the idea of confiding in me?

'Come here, from now on I'm batting for the other side!' My friend got up and stood in front of me swaying back and forward, she made an attempt to embrace me but fell full force into me.

I assumed she had not had a drink for a while. That night I heard Ayane and Luc giving it their all in the bedroom next to mine. I felt embarrassed and excited at the same time. Never before had it occurred to me how similar the sounds of mating were to the sounds of being in pain.

'Oh, and I've given your question some thought.' I always did this. I would witter away, picking at some trivial dribs and drabs, free floating nonsense would fill the space and the time of our session. Then, when it was almost time to go, I'd come up with something real.

'The guilt-question?'

I smiled sourly. 'Yes, the guilt-question.' She too smiled.

'We had a massive row last week, Raf and I.' She nodded, she was expecting this.

'More than a row, really, more a sort of 'Who's afraid of Virginia Woolf'-war, full of blame and bile. I'm not even sure there is a way back.' She didn't say: *there is always a way back.*

'Would you want that?'

'What? A way back?'

Her question took me by surprise. I looked at her, the answer would come to me in a minute. Neither of us said anything for a while. I studied the varnish on my nails. They could do with another coat. 'I really don't know.' Again, my therapist nodded and looked at me, unmoved. I started to feel at ease.

'I have said terrible things to him, more or less accused him of everything.'

'Of everything?'

'Of the loss of my daughter.'

'That's serious.'

'I know. Was that cruel of me?'

'It is clearly what you feel, Emma. Sometimes it is cruel to say what you feel, indeed. But I suspect you think it cruel because in reality things are far more complicated and perhaps not merely a matter of guilt.'

This time it was I who nodded. My nose had started to prickle, I would not be able to hold back my tears much longer. She delicately pushed the box of tissues closer to me. For a moment I resented the clichéd shrink association, but despite everything this felt good. The crying and the talking to someone who was able to deal with it and prepared to show me around in my own head.

'You said this happened last week.'

'Yes.'

'How have things been between you since?'

I shrugged my shoulders. 'Search me. We pretend nothing has happened. That is to say, Raf does.'

'Is that usually the pattern, after a confrontation?'

'I suppose it is, yes.' I looked at the clock. I had exactly three minutes left. 'I'm generally the one who wishes to revisit the outburst. Raf usually tells me straight away that there is no point, regardless of the seriousness of the fight. He'll knock it on the head with an *it's all just part and parcel of being in a relationship.*'

'How does that make you feel?' She glanced at the clock, ever so discreetly.

'How does that make me feel? On the one hand I feel, I can't quite explain, it's very mixed in fact. On the one hand there is disappointment, realising we obviously can't move on like that. Nothing is ever going to change if we can't learn from our falls, is it? We're bound to perpetually relapse.'

'And on the other hand? Relief?'

'Yes. Relief. For sure. The whole thing is so very wearing, all those reoccurring frictions and crashes. Those same old dialogues, over and over and over again, that banal, hysterical record of ours, one utterly worn at that.'

'Can we take this up again next week, Emma? Your feelings of ambivalence about conflict resolution in your relationship with Raf?'

'Raf?'

'Mmm? They're quite all right you know, those prices for Santiago flights.'

'Raf?' He finally looked up from his screen. 'Yes?'

'Can we talk?' He stared at me as if I proposed to head into town bollock-naked.

'What do you mean?'

'A little chat. About last week.' I made it smaller.

He looked at me, then at his keyboard, a tormented expression on his face.

'Come on, Em, not again.'

'What do you mean, again? Did I miss something?'

'We were purely letting off steam last week, that's all. We were both angry and unreasonable.'

'Unreasonable? Or did we finally tell it how it is?'

'See? Now we're off again, is that what you want? Well, I don't, I'm off to bed.'

'All right then, let it all ferment again, be my guest.' When he reached the stairs, he turned round to face me. 'What exactly is it you want from me, Emma? That I come along to this shrink of yours? To turn all my feelings and intentions inside out? To correct my inadequate ways? To dissect our joint shit?' He looked pleased with his improvised lines. His voice had been on its way up to its highest register.

'Oh, surely not that. We're much better off suffocating in this shit of ours, aren't we? That shows true dignity, doesn't it? Never mind, Raf.' I waved my hand, indicating that I had given up.

Raf walked up the stairs. I could hear him switch on the bathroom lights, brush his teeth, take a pee and switch off the lights again. He did not walk onto the bedroom but took up position on the landing, most likely he was leaning over the banister. Funny how one becomes such an expert in decoding small domestic noises.

'Em?'

'What?'

'Come to bed soon, ok?' A reconciliation phrase.

'I'm just going to sit here for a bit. I won't be too long.' We had escaped a new fight, but how long for? Or would I, like him, gradually become better at denial? Would I give up expecting the impossible? But how was I to marry our respective versions of the truth? Or did that not even matter? I poured myself another glass of wine and stretched out on the sofa. Had I secretly hoped for this result? Had I provoked a conversation which I knew he would decline? What good did my own endless analyses do? Whatever it was, I needed this, a moment to myself, Raf-less relaxing. I closed my eyes and surrendered to the story that I had warmed myself with for the last few days.

Carefully I slid into the bed next to Raf and pulled the sheet a bit towards me. It was too warm for the duvet. There seemed to be no end to this late summer heat. It was as if it needed to burn off the humidity of the previous wet months. We'd had had no summer to speak of, which had suited me just fine. Days on end I had spent in pyjamas on the settee, the soft ticking of the rain on the windows, like a soothing melody. No cheerful, flowery summer dresses over sun tanned legs for me, no drinks on terraces, no romantic evening walks through the centre of the old town.

Raf's hand gently caressed my back, my thighs, my bottom. Shit: he was still awake. He moved closer to me and kissed my shoulder and my neck. I stayed where I was, on my tummy.

I then turned to face him. We kissed. Raf stretched his arm to reach the bed side lamp. 'No, don't.'

'No?'

'No, nice and cool and dark. Do you mind?'

'Not at all, pumpkin, I can feel how gorgeous you are.' His hand was fondling my belly, my legs, it slid in between them. 'Hmm, lovely girl of mine, how wet you are.' Again, Joris's face appeared.

Expecting was a mixed bag.

It was hoping and fearing all at the same time.

The fear was about the unknown, projected onto an infinite spectrum of concrete potential disasters. The hope was about the desire to believe and the illusion that this positive energy had the power to influence the outcome. To hope was to begin.

I now had to find a new beginning, as though I had lost the end of a messed-up bobbin of cotton.

What I missed most about the entire pregnancy cult, apart from the radical state of expectation, was pissing on sticks.

Few mundane actions resulted in a more immediate shock wave than a *Clearblue*-pee: a breath-taking, godly, crystal-clear line. Pregnancy sticks were life's ultimate tombola, the stark blue starter mark where it would all begin, or the finishing line that signalled the end of a promise. I had done it everywhere.

In supermarket toilets straight after purchase, the packaging of the clairvoyant device hastily torn open. In lavatories at airports, theatres and restaurants, in Raf's grandmother's dinky powder room, secretly in the woods, on a bucket in a tent. At home I kept a supply and most days I would carry a first aid wee-kit in my handbag. I could read my own body like a book: swollen bosoms and minimal discharge around the time of a period could indicate success. Monthly periods slightly over due, darkened aureole: *Clearblue* would provide certainty or at least a window of several minutes of hope. A friend once told me you could get addicted to almost anything. He was right and I was living proof of this: *My name is Emma and I'm addicted to 'Clearblue'*. No past tense, for my supply still lay waiting, tantalisingly, if redundant, in the top drawer with my knickers

Luc's theory proved to be right. To a certain extent working with children dulled the pain of not having them. I wasn't one of those women who wanted a child because she was being denied her right to have one. Or had I ceased to be? I had never felt I was entitled to a child, I had wanted one but been unlucky. As Luc had rightly observed, inhabiting a child's world came naturally to me. I felt blessed with their spontaneous cuddles and unedited chatter, with their sticky hands and runny noses. I was learning to accept, even if I regularly regressed into my old patterns of indignation and self-pity. My grieving process, like any other, went through stages. I courageously climbed my mountain of mourning, to find that every new plateau offered me a fresh outlook on my wound. No doubt my perspective would keep on transforming. There would come a time when I would envy my friends their grandchildren. My therapist encouraged me to face this fear and voice it.

I had the feeling Joris was attracted to me. He would often seek out my company and had offered to help me out with Wednesday rehearsals. Both about my work and my looks he was openly flattering. 'Such an infectious laughter you have, miss Em', he said one morning when I stood giggling in the corridor with a few children from the cast. 'I'd join in without knowing why, really.' Another time I was on the stage, busy painting white dots on giant red mushrooms. Joris approached me and offered to help. I told him I was as good as finished. *Did I know there was an Alice buzz all over the playground? All who weren't part of drama club were deemed uncool.* 'How do you do this?' I smiled at him and looked away, my cheeks started to burn. 'By the way, like the hair. Very Mia Farrow.' I rushed into the wings with my little bucket of paint *busy, busy, busy, sorry*, my head as red as one of my mushroom props.

The hair cut had been the stage one in what was to become my big metamorphoses. Pristine look, new purpose, fresh life juices. Or at least that was Ayane's vision. Raf thought the disappearance of my long, blond locks a pity. Why not just try another cut? His remark had encouraged me to go for it: my life, my body and me in charge.

Joris and I had had a few intimate talks at a school's party and in the pub after a rehearsal and one too many drinks.

'How long have you been separated?' Joris sat at the table opposite me, he was swearing into his mobile phone, his ex-wife's au pair had hers switched off. 'Three years and a bit. Some things remain tricky. Or rather, the kids remain tricky.'

'Yes, I can imagine. How old are they?'

He slid the phone back into the inside pocket of his jacket. 'Jeanne is six, Thijs three and a half.'

'Nice names.' Joris nodded absently.

'How about you? May I ask?'

'You may, but be aware of what you're getting into.'

I wasn't sure what meant myself. I had wanted to sound mysterious and witty, air my heart with its door ajar, flirt with my boss, free of consequences, without betraying Raf.

'Oh dear, that bad?'

'It's a long story, Mr Durrant.' I had gone on to sketch the outlines of our fertility hell. In between the lines I had hinted that all this had put quite a bit of strain on our relationship. It didn't often happen that I was so unguarded with someone I did not know well. But I remained cautious; there was a palpable erotic tension between us and I suspected he'd take the bait as soon as I'd hold it out to him. 'What are you reading?' The book was partly sticking out of my bag, which lay on the table between us. It was a whopper, but I couldn't help dragging it along wherever I went. Every spare moment I found myself returning to the bold confessions of the protagonist of this gripping, confessional novel. Eva was a woman with an underdeveloped maternal instinct, who felt guilty about the fact she had, despite this, embarked on motherhood and was now left wondering to what extent her own inadequacy had triggered her son's derailment. Brave and controversial, the novel traced the ultimate nature-nurture debate. I pushed my thumbed copy of Lionel Shriver's 'We need to talk about Kevin' towards Joris.

'You're kidding!'

'What?'

Joris dived under the table and fished a slightly less battered copy of the book out of his brief case. 'Oh my God, this is spooky!' We both laughed in disbelief. 'And? You addicted too?'

'Are you joking? Why do you think I've got it on me? A lukewarm reader like myself would normally leave a book at home, on the bedside cabinet, where it belongs. This thing, however, gets to follow me around *ever-y-where*: to lunch, to the toilet, back to the office, where I balance it on the desk next to my laptop, flung open in order to devour a secret little paragraph in between emails, or to pinch a guilty page after a draining meeting; I've even considered hiding it on my lap *during*, but realised even I couldn't get away with that.

I nodded and smiled. 'Phenomenal, don't you think?'

'Absolutely. So recognisable.'

'What is?'

'Oh, lots of things. The unrelenting battle between parents about accountability, responsibility, consistency. The guilt trips, the constant attacks on the other's way of dealing with things, or not dealing with things, whatever, this utterly wearing, eroding, toxic couple dynamic, often with a child powerless at the heart of it all. But in this case, with a manipulative, cold hearted creep at the heart, orchestrating it all, exploiting this division, driving his parents discord to a crescendo. Gruesome. But brilliant. Just brilliant.'

'Wow, you've thought about this! But you're so right, Joris. She captures that tension like no other, I agree.' I had picked up his copy and tried to gauge where he had his bookmark.

'Oh, how funny, that we're both reading this. Where are you?'

'She is pregnant again. How about you?' I felt like saying that unfortunately I wasn't, but was able to stop myself. 'At the very end, don't worry, I won't give anything away. Have you read other stuff by her?'

'No. You?'

'Yes, an earlier novel called 'Double Fault.'

'And?'

'Equally sublime, although the reviews weren't that good. Again, she focuses on the battle of the sexes, but this time with a little bit more subtlety, incredibly profound.

Strong language, like in Kevin, visceral dialogues, funny too, ironic, but merciless all the same. Brilliant observations, again of the power battles in a relationship and how they shift and how they in the end destroy what made the couple work in the first place, you know?'

'I *do* know. I'll have to read it, it's my story!'

'It's most people's story, Joris,' I said wryly. 'Will you have another? Same again, Duvel?'

'Definitely.' Joris got up and dug a twenty euro note up from the back pocket of his trousers. 'It's fine,' I said.

'Don't you dare, this is my round.'

'You do need to be careful with these things, you know.'

'How do you mean?'

'I have the feeling you are leading him on, Emma.' Ayane always cycled with one hand. She sat bolt upright and gracefully pushed the pedals. She could not help it, she was elegant at whatever she did.

'No, absolutely not! We click, that's all, which is great.'

'Yea, whatever.' She looked at me, then away from me, a few times. She wasn't buying it.

'He's forever paying you compliments, you hang out in the pub together, you're passionate about the same books and it seems you barely need words to know what the other one means or feels. Jesus, Em, you have erotic dreams about the man. Handy, isn't it, that he happens to be a divorcee?'

'Don't be ridiculous, Aya. I am not though, am I?'

'No. That's right. Not yet.'

'What's that supposed to mean?'

'That you're playing with fire and you know it. You're using me as your touchstone. Or did you want to deny that too?'

I cycled on more fiercely.

'Emma! Can you wait for me, for God's sake?' We arrived at the entrance of *Middelheim Park* where we stalled and locked our bikes.

Ayane spread out the table cloth. She stoically began to transfer our lunch from her basket on to the cloth on the lawn. I stood looking at her, wondering what had made her so upset. Were things not what they seemed between her and Luc and did she herself toy with adulterous thoughts? Or did she sincerely stick up for Raf, for whom she felt all the more since he was not in a position to defend himself?

'How will I ever know that with certainty, Aya, that things are over between us? Is this not how it usually goes in relationship battles? People try to hang on for the longest of time, forcing their crooked pact straight again, making themselves believe that the frictions and frustrations will soon subside, that with a bit of genuine attention to one another a crash can be diverted. A matter of rebooting the machine, simple as that. We're all so desperate to believe we're not alone in this, as though that somehow matters. That it's one of those critical phases every long-term relationship goes through. And all the while there isn't a word or a look or a touch of the other that doesn't give you the creeps. Then one day you bump into someone. You allow that person into your heart and all of the sudden everything accelerates. Is that not how things go, when two people decide to call it a day after a gruelling tug of war? What if this guy turns out to be the love of my life? Is that not possible?'

'Of course that's possible. But I don't think your sequence of events is kosher. Nor is your timing. *Love of my life*. Honestly, you have no idea what you're doing.'

'What is it I'm doing, Ayane?'

'What I said: you're playing with matches. Next thing you know you're surrounded by flames wondering what the hell happened.'

I sighed. Was she right? Was the theory I was trying to sell to her despicable? Had I secretly written off Raf already and was Joris reeling me in as he showered me with his attention? No. Things were not this banal. I was not that cheap. But it was a fact that I was desperately worn out by our quarrels and by my own obstinate part in this.

'Lately I have the feeling my mouth is set in this bitter line, the corners turned down and it scares me, you know that? It's an Emma I don't recognise and one I definitely don't wish to be. I'm not playing with fire, but you are my touchstone, that's true, my sounding board, my conscience even.' Ayane looked into her paper cup.

'Perhaps I simply need to air all this,' I went on. 'To hear what my own thoughts sound like and to have you bounce them back to me, with notes in the margins. Angry notes, and entire passages crossed out. Something like that, anyway.'

'Yes, something like that.' Ayane had a pained look on her face. 'Don't you think I have moments like this, Emma? And clicks with fascinating, available men?'

'I have no idea. You don't tell me, do you?'

'No. And I wouldn't dream of airing it either. Or articulating it, as your lady-shrink likes to put it, no doubt to make it sound less threatening. No one will deny that day dreaming can be fun, healthy even, a bit like trying out stuff in your head first. But feeding your dreams can make you reckless. You either try out a new track with Raf or you leave him. *Then* explore the world out there. Or your boss's bed, for all I care.'

Ayane's advice kept going through my head for the rest of that week. On one hand I found her uncompromising views reassuring, on the other hand they seemed too simple.
She was right, day dreams did have a function, as did flirting and opening up to someone's advances.

Open-up! What if it was the magic formula which would allow old choices to be traded in for new ones, the risk taker's attitude that would bring about change? Was my opening up a first step to taking my life in my own hands?

Ayane urged me to act with moral integrity, there was nothing I wanted more. For months I had tried to build a new pathway with Raf, but I felt there was no point as long as the old, broken tracks could not be unearthed.

'Happy birthday, love.' Raf pushed the bedroom door open with his foot. He was carrying a tray, on it a steaming cafetière, a carafe of juice, croissants and a small bowl of raspberries, my favourite fruit.

'*Rafke*, how sweet!'

He put down the tray, poured out a glass of juice and handed it to me. He kissed my forehead. I took a sip. 'Mmm, very nice.'

'Here.' From the pocket of his bathrobe he took a brown envelope that had my name on it.

'What is this?'

'Open it.'

'Eurostar tickets? To go where? Gosh, London, brilliant!'

'The Easter weekend after 'Alice', I hope that's ok, if it isn't, that's not a problem, I can always cancel and rebook, just let me...'

'No. It's perfect.'

'Really?'

'Absolutely.'

'Oh, and I've reserved a quirky little guest house in Greenwich, in south east London.'

'I know it, yes, but I've never been. *Greenwich meantime*, of the prime meridian, is that right?'

'It is. Apparently, it's very arty, lots of cosy pubs and eateries and trendy little shops. And obviously there's tons of naval history and a famous park as well, Greenwich Park with the Royal Observatory. That's where you can stand with one foot in the east and one in the west. There's a well-known crafts market too, right up your street.'

'Very exciting.'

'You can actually take a boat from Greenwich to the centre of London, to Westminster, I thought you'd like that. It even has its own theatre, did you know that? Often Greenwich theatre attracts big names, we could look into that and book a show, what do you say?'

Raf was getting completely carried away by his pre-tour-guide chatter.

'Come here.' I pulled the worn lapels of Raf's battered robe towards me. A life-time ago this garment had been synonymous with weekend harmony, with long drawn out brunches and bare feet on the patio, with not getting dressed yet or showered.

Once, long ago, the guilty pleasure of postponing the start of the day had been part of the fabric of our scruffy bath robes, which smelled of excitement, sex, possibility.

I so wanted to believe I could forgive him. That there would be life after our wars and new forms of hope, even if I had no clue whether or not he was to be part of this. I kissed him.

'It's a wonderful present, Raf. Thanks a lot.'

'What do you mean, no soap?'

'Nope. No shampoo, no towels and no soap.'

'You're not serious?'

'I think you need to go back downstairs, Raf and ask her...'

'No way! I'm not asking that woman anything; she gives me the creeps.' I sashayed towards him in my jeans and bra. 'Youwa shuwar your nat staying langa, sirr?'

'Jesus Em, I'm sorry. I've booked us a brothel!'

'Mister need no soap. Mister from Holland. Dirty peepul. Yes?'

I knelt in front of him and started to undo his fly.

Raf's quirky Greenwich pension turned out to be to be a seedy curry joint in Charlton, with screaming wall paper and a filthy carpet, run by a Thai woman, caked in make-up, wearing a see-through negligee. The place was permeated by a stale tobacco smell, with a sharp spicy undertone and even though there was a small sash window in our bedroom, it was permanently jammed and could only be forced open a centimetre or two. Yet somehow this shabby, almost decadent atmosphere excited me.

'Greenwich village is at least a forty-five-minute walk from here, Em.' Raf came out of the shower. Or rather: he came out from the corner near the drain hole, opposite the toilet, where he had held the shower hose over his head and attempted a soap-free wash. After all, this was the *wet room* from the website, which had only offered a picture of the one acceptable aspect of the house, its front. Raf dried himself with a T-shirt.

'That's all right, it's a nice day. Besides *Greenwich Village* is in New York, babe. Here they just call it Greenwich, although apparently the locals say 'Grinnidge'. Now it was me who was quoting the rough guide, sprawled on our pension-bed, dreamy after an unusually horny fuck.

'Some of these Indian restaurants get four stars, you know? There's even a Vietnamese here with five stars, right in the centre, near that boat, you know, the old sea clipper, *The Cutty Sark*?'

'Sounds good.'

'Oh, no.'

'What?'

'The boat is currently closed for repairs, it says here. Seems there was a fire a while back. Oh, that's a shame. However, it does look as if we can get to the centre of Greenwich via the park, but you're right, it's a fair walk, but not three quarters of an hour, more like half an hour, if you ask me. Raf came over to the bed and kissed the top of my head. 'This was a good idea, wasn't it? I mean, London, not the brothel.' I looked into his eyes. He looked older, lately, more worried. He had started to lose his hair. The communication with Marie was strained. After years of unconditional father adoration, which was no doubt intended to create a wedge between her dad and me, she had now joined the hostile mother camp and reproached Raf for all that was wrong in her young life.

'One of your better ones, *Rafke*, whorehouse and all. Come and lie with me for a bit. This scruffy bed is exceptionally comfortable. Perhaps we need to take a nap before we start exploring '*Grinnidge.*'

'Absolutely brilliant. I have rarely been so blown away by a play, honestly.' I found myself checking Raf's animated expression; was he pulling my leg?

'I'm serious, Emma. At one point I even had goose bumps.' From behind my wine glass I was nodding in agreement, as I leafed through the programme. I was equally speechless after this gripping performance of Eugene O'Briens *Eden*, a play I had not known when I booked it on-line almost two months ago.

'You did know this play, right? Or did you not? How did you find it?'

'I knew *of* it, yes. I did a bit of research, read a couple of reviews, looked at some other shows in London but fancied this one more than the rest. It sounded dark, yet funny. Very Irish, which always attracts me, obviously, the accent, the themes, you know.' Unlike Raf, I had no problem with accents. During the play I had tried to keep him up to speed, although he had seemed engrossed enough, despite his linguistic limitations. A long time ago, before I met Raf, I had been on a tour around Ireland with an award-winning Becket adaptation; I had very warm memories of those days and kept a fondness for all things Irish.

'I cannot put my finger on it, why it should move me like it did. But it did.'

'It's the powerlessness, isn't it? The emotional impotence, you know? The wanting more, the feeling that there's perhaps something missing. Ultimately, it's about the torture of choice, isn't it? A bit like that Paul Simon line: *the thought that life could be better is woven indelibly into our hearts and our brains.*'

'Yes. There is definitely that.' Raf sat with his chin in his hands, eyes staring into space. I knew he was wandering back to what had so moved him out there on the stage and that he was looking for words to communicate it to me. I felt warm towards him.

'These are monologues about inarticulacy,' I read from the brochure. *'Not being able to talk, to fuck, to be married.'* As if it suddenly all became a bit too much, Raf stood up. 'Another large white?' I smiled and nodded, as he walked towards the packed theatre bar. It was Saturday night. The Arts Theatre was in the heart of London, near Leicester Square. We had spent the afternoon meandering around, first in Greenwich, then at the other side of London in Kew Gardens. Finally, we had taken a train back to London Bridge in order to visit the Tate Modern. We'd even had dinner there, with magical views over the Millennium Bridge to St Pauls Cathedral. I had enjoyed every minute. For the first time in ages there was no tension between us, just carefree enjoyment, which I could scarcely believe. On my shoulder Ayane was looking on, egging me on: 'Bloody hell, Emma, you cynical beast, go for it, ok?'

Raf and I stayed in the bar a while longer. From Billy and Breda, we seamlessly switched to good old Emma and Raf and whatever might be left of their contract. And then I asked him, finally, almost exactly eleven months later, in that buzzing theatre bar in London, after three large glasses of wine, I asked him.
'Raf?'
'Yes?'
'Have you ever regretted the amniocentesis?' At first, he looked me blankly in the eye, his face a frozen computer screen, there was no way I'd get it to work for a while.
This surely was the last thing he'd expected of our patch-up weekend away. He kept staring at me in complete silence.
'Emma', he said. It sounded like *shit*. Like *what-the-fuck.* Like *why do you always have to.* But then he seemed to have a change of heart. He took my hand in his and gently squeezed it, his eyes averted. Was that genuine or tactical? How was one ever to know? Was it important?
'Yes.'
'Yes?'
'Of course I have. How could I not? Like you I have to live on, wondering if our child could have been alive now, if we hadn't... if *I* hadn't insisted on the amnio. But I'm just as pained by this hypothetical uncertainty, not knowing if my girl, our girl, six months old this week, would be healthy. Would have been, I mean. Do you want to know what I find the worst about all this?'
'What?'

'That I don't know what tortures me most, her not being there or her not being healthy. I know, I have no way of picturing, imagining any of this, it makes no sense whatsoever, but I can't stop myself. I can't stop that film. Over and over again I have the most gruesome scenarios popping up and I feel paralysed and sick to the stomach, yet none of it makes me feel as awkward, as inept as I did on that day. Us two, on either side of the fence.'

A teardrop fell on to the back of my hand, which was resting on his. Raf wiped his runny nose with his free hand, I pulled mine away and dried my own eyes. I did not want to say what I was thinking: all the signs had indicated that we were going to have a healthy baby. We were having a healthy girl. No, we *had* her, this girl in the making. Why did you need to edit the story in your head? Because this was the only way for you to deal with it? I stroked his arm.

'We were asked to play God and that's what we will have to live with. It's just, I cannot allow this too often, Emma, I don't work like that. If you force me to then…I will break, we will break, do you know what I'm saying?'

'I'm sorry.' It had left my lips with hardly a sound, one hand in front of my eyes, the other around a wet ball of tissue, pressed against my mouth.

He had called her his girl and had not meant Marie. She lived in months and days in his tormented head, where she wasn't dead, though possibly bruised. Suddenly there was an overpowering desire to know her, to name her. Never again would I force Raf to share his vision of her with me. I was not going to break him.

Arm in arm we headed for Charing Cross station where we just about caught the last train to Greenwich. The next morning, on the Eurostar with bagels and coffee, I felt at ease confessing to Raf that the thought of a world trip with him rather oppressed me. I told him about Ayane's invitation. I told him that I liked the idea of spending time with her and Luc and that I even warmed to the prospect of beach fun with Tamako and Takuya.

Part 3

The sun rose over Olbia. We were on our way to the holiday villa in a rental car, all four of us feeling worn out but elated. Tamako's sleepy head was lying in my lap, mine was resting on Raf's shoulder. Luc was behind the wheel. Next to him Ayane was trying her best to calm down her youngest, who was screeching and wriggling like a frenzied spider monkey. Takuya and his sister had been as good as gold during the late flight from Brussels. Now the boy seemed determined to punish the adults for disturbing his routine.

I was fond of travel fatigue, of jet lag even. I felt in airports and during flights one had an almost surreal sense of time. Doing a spot of shopping, having breakfast or aperitif at three in the morning was suddenly normal, as though one were operating in a void of borrowed time, outside real time. I knew it did not make sense, but in this rule free non-time interval I felt less responsible, a bit like a sleepwalker driven by a power beyond my control.

Last summer Luc and Ayane had rented this same house. Little Takuya had only been two months old.

And there it was: the villa from the pictures. I suddenly remembered how I had to press my friend to show them to me. A week or two after their holiday I happened to notice Ayane's screen saver: a beaming, bare-bottomed Takauya in the arms of his glowing mother, out on the terrace of their bougainvillea clad Sardinian villa, against the backdrop of a perfect sky.

'They're nothing special, you know, Luc keeps taking these same pictures over and over again.' What was going through her mother-Theresa-head this time? *Can't shove the poor girl's nose into our idyllic holiday snaps, can I? Sun, sand and sea and chirpy toddler on proud daddy's shoulders, divine newly born curled up in the cot, in the pergola's shade... stunning villa by the bay?* Obviously, I had been overcome by a confusion of emotions, but my attempts to conquer bouts of envy and to come across as genuinely enthusiastic, had become one of my life's tasks.
In those days Raf used to take great pleasure in reading moral superiority into my so-called martyr's role, whenever we had a spat. In those days I wanted to run away from his sarcastic, scrutinising gaze. Now I felt his hand on my leg, giving it a little squeeze. 'Look, Em, we're here. Christ, what a mansion!'

'No way! Are you sure?'

My objections can't have sounded very convincing as Ayane insisted: Raf and I were to share the master bedroom with luxury on suite bath room and adjacent balcony with sea views to die for. I opened the sliding doors and could smell the sea. The first bathers were already strolling in the direction of playa Isuledda to claim their spot for the day. My friend explained it was handier for her and Luc to have the room next to Tamako's, at the back of the house, with views almost just as delightful over the gardens. Besides, that room was better equipped for the baby. Fourteen months old now and solidly walking, Takuya remained 'the baby'.

Two days after his first birthday he had started to walk. It had not felt like a coincidence that I had been there and that they had led to me and my inviting arms, those first hesitant, weighty steps of his, accompanied by the boy's signature crow, high and monotonous, like a cracked whistle. Luc called it his Taekwondo-roar. The funniest thing was that his little face remained deadly serious, as if the scream were merely a matter of, literally, letting off steam as he set off on this precarious endeavour that needed all of his concentration. With so much expression in his voice, there was clearly none left for his face. Once safe and sound arrived in my arms, the summit of his very own Everest, my godson took great pleasure in receiving the acclaim and surrendering to a top-class cuddle. As he relaxed, his victorious mouth and flat little eyes faded into ironed out, horizontal lines.

Takuya was an incredibly tactile child. Whenever he was being read a story, be it by his parents, his uncle Raf or me, a little hand or foot would invariably creep up to a warm body part of the reader. It never felt clingy, it was a mere manifestation of Takuya's insatiable need to touch. Tamako was affectionate too, but as far as the need for physical closeness went, the baby definitely had the edge.

The next morning, we were all out on the terrace for breakfast. Luc had gone out at the crack of dawn to stock up for food. The children looked animated and rested. Takuya was banging his plastic beaker on the table full force in a wordless request for more milk; around his mischievous grin were the chocolate outlines of an extra mouth. The four adults, all but for Luc still in pyjamas, were joking and chatting and hugging their coffees, a picture of holiday relaxation. Beneath us to the left, at the bottom of the stairs leading from the terrace to the patio, the blue water of our very own private pool was mirroring the sun in playful little circles. Ahead of us, a vast, clear blue sky sat on top of the aquamarine mass that was the sea. Even from here we were able to make out the tiny white heads of foam as they hit an almost deserted beach.

In the coming days it would become our biggest dilemma: whether to all head for the beach, laden with snacks and snorkels and buckets and spades or to nestle by the side of the pool with sunscreen, inflatables, mags and books and to take it in turn to supervise the kids?

Our repeated discussions about this were ludicrous. Playa Isuledda was a mere five minutes' walk from the house. Was the problem the off-putting thought of having to go back to the villa to fetch a forgotten item? Or was there no problem, but simply an attachment to having to sort something out, to find one voice as a group? Often our party would split up anyway. Sometimes Ayane and I would go to the beach in the morning with one of the children, or with both, while Raf and Luc stayed in the house or took a spin out in the car. At other times it would be Tamako or Takuya who stayed with the men. From time to time Raf and I would go for a late afternoon walk or a siesta. On one occasion both children stayed with Raf and Luc for Ayane and I to enjoy a careless girly day out.

After breakfast Luc was to drive us to the centre of San Teodoro. The plan was that we would gorge ourselves in the local boutiques, have small breaks for coffee or ice cream, shop some more and stop somewhere for a light lunch. Late afternoon we would take a cab to Coda Cavallo and have drinks and dinner in the Blue Bar, to the breath-taking view over Punte Est and the peninsula.

Ayane sighed and sampled her cocktail. 'This, my precious, is what it's all about. Sun, sea, booze and new sexy sandals and no one but my bosom pal to witness so much guilty pleasure.'

'How so, guilty?'

'No, I'm only joking. I could get used to these husband-and-kid-free outings. But there definitely is an uneasy feeling, as if I'm doing something terribly naughty and I'm being pulled back by invisible wires attached to my ears.'

'What on earth are you taking about? You drunk already? I think there's only one person pulling you back and that's you.'

'You're probably right. It feels great and the fun does make up for the earache.'

Ayane leant forward and kissed my cheek, there was almost a suggestion of tears in her eyes. 'Thank you, *Emmetje*. Thanks for today and thanks for coming on this holiday with us.'

'That's a good one, she's thanking *me*.' I held up my Bellini.

Aynane raised hers. 'To us, my darling, to our friendship. For ever and a day.'

I took a sip. 'That is very long, isn't it?' My cynical voice was never lost for long.

'It is indeed.' She gave me a stern stare. 'You have a better offer then?' I started laughing. I felt pleasantly tired; the warm glow of the heady concoction was hitting the spot. I rubbed my friend's bare thigh. Ayane was wearing a shockingly short purple skirt. Only she could pull this off without a hint of vulgarity; she always managed to look like Bowie's little China girl. *Shhh. Oh, baby just you shut your mouth.* 'I love you, do you know that? My precious little oriental mascot, I really do.' Ayane relaxed back into the cushions of the deep swivel chair and crossed her long brown legs. In an exaggerated move she began kicking the sandaled foot of her crossed leg as she held my gaze. The heels were immense, I would keel over in those.

'Oh, babe, they look so good on you. Proper classy.' I stroked the thin silver strap that stretched over her toes with my index finger. Set in the leather was a delicate band of tiny shells and mother of pearl sequins. On the ankle strap the pattern was repeated in a slight variation.

'Top purchase. Definitely worth the money. That husband of yours is going to be seriously turned on when you show up in these.'

'No kidding.' Ayane raised her eye brows.

'What? Don't you think so?'

'Oh, I'm sure he will, love. As long as he can keep his eyes open that is and even then. Let's just say that man of mine is not really a shoe-fetishist.'

'Oh well, you were set on bagging an earthy Fleming, weren't you?

'What about Raf? Can he get excited about stuff like that?'

'Raf? You're kidding, aren't you? If I were to ask him if I should wear army boots to my salsa class he would reply *Why not?*'

'I know. They're never really looking, are they, once you've bagged them as you put it.'

'Let's simply admit we're doing it for ourselves. Or for unknown men.'

'Is that so?'

'No, of course not. Although I do think it's about being seen. Being noticed by others. Men, women, third parties of any description.'

'And why is that?' Ayane popped an olive in her mouth. She really did look like a young girl in her mum's high heels.

'To catch your own reflection in their eyes? Something like that? To have your deepest feminine self caressed by the gaze of the outside world? What do I know? I'm just talking crap.'

'I don't think you are. You have a point. All of this is very primitive, right? What's the point of tempting the one you've already bagged? From an evolutionary point of view, it's a waste of energy, right? Your nest is filled already.'

'If you're lucky, yes.'

'Sorry. I didn't mean it like that.'

'Then how did you mean it?'

'Emma, I merely wanted to point out...'

'It's fine, honestly. And I get your point. I'm wondering if it explains my urge to wander, you know, every now and then, away from the empty nest.'

'Emma, please.'

'Oh, here we go. You're sounding like Raf now, so these kinds of observations are taboo, are they?'

'Not at all Emma, they're not taboo.' She looked away from me. 'Sorry, you're right, if you can't be honest around me then, where can you?'

We looked out over the sea in silence.

'I love him, you know, Raf, I know that more than ever now. I think I sobered up a bit about what you can expect of the other in a long-term relationship. I'm a bit more aware of the need for ongoing renegotiation. I guess it's a question of bending or breaking. But I too feel a pull, from time to time Aya, but mine's in the other direction. The itch to get away, to find out if this is it or if there's more out there, somewhere. I don't necessarily mean getting away from Raf, that's almost not the point. Sometimes I have the feeling that the dreams we chase are a lot more random than we like to think or like to admit to ourselves. What does it mean to love someone once you've lost the glue of your common goal? When you're no longer looking in the same direction, things need redefining, right?'

'Oh, God, Emma. For as long as I've known you you've had doubts about who you are and where you are going.'

'That may be so, but as a mother I would not have been able to afford that.'

'Is that what you think?'

'I do believe kids anchor you, yes.'

'Bullshit.'

'Oh. OK.' I was surprised by the fierceness of her reaction.

78

'The best you can hope for is that all this inner turmoil does not mess with your presence as a mum. It's not as though you get an existential bypass when you give birth, Em. Of course, there are Madame Bovarys and Ana Kareninas, women who don't find an anchor in motherhood, on the contrary. But you would not have flipped, Emma, I'm almost certain of that. But motherhood alone would not have made you any less restless either. Believe me, you would have remained who you are, with all those whimsical ups and downs of yours, mother or not. And a good one at that. It seems to me you're looking for a bonus for your childlessness, a beneficial by-product. It seems to help you to believe that the mere fact of having a child would have compromised your moral integrity.'

I looked at my friend, dismayed, I felt caught out. There was only one phrase from her discourse I wanted to take away: *a good one at that.* Ayane believed I would have been a good mum. All the rest was what it was, Ayanishly insightful and wise.

The sun was starting to slip behind the hills. It gave the sea deck a golden glow. It was getting late but we were in no hurry, the men had given us carte blanche. For all they cared we'd return to the house in the early hours of the morning. The taxi that had brought us to Coda Cavallo would pick us up and drive us to the villa.

'Do you mean that?'

'What?'

'That I'd have made a good mother.'

'For two hundred percent.'

'How pathetic is that? That it matters to me? Hypothetically matters.'

'That is by no means pathetic, you silly sod.' I laughed about her use of words. I laughed because I was relieved. Everyone seemed to think I had accepted my loss, that it was a closed chapter. In my commitment to other people's children I appeared to have found a calling or at least a sense of purpose. My own feelings were much more ambivalent. I was relatively contented with my life but in everything I undertook, whether it be with Ayane's children or the little actors of my company, the stigma of self-pity was attached to my retina; through my own eyes I saw myself operate like a pitiable mother derivative. I couldn't help wondering how I would have done 'for real'. My dedication to other people's kids was genuine and false at the same time. The greediness with which it filled my void was poignant.

Was all this part of my *closure* or was I acting a part? My main enemy was this merciless, relentless self-analysis.

'That won't stop Em, it won't, ever.'

'Never ever ever?' I fought the tears as I played jokey-Em.

'I don't think so, no. I think there's a void there that won't go away. A hole inside. But there is something else there too; your ability to give and to *be*, to be warm, there's an immense potential, an inexhaustible creative craving and longing and wanting, that lives there too, inside of you.' Ayane had the tendency to get carried away by her own florid descriptions. She'd sail on this wave of metaphors, where all her thoughts were connected and sounded like the chorus of a Greek tragedy, or a Disney theme.

'Some hole.'

My friend got up and came to sit next to me on the wooden window seat. She teasingly started to shake me, holding me by the shoulders. 'Some treasure box I've got there.' It wasn't funny but I suddenly felt like being silly. Ayane tickled my sides, I collapsed. 'Aya, stop it, people are watching!'

All of a sudden, she sat up right, poised, decent, smoothing her skirt. She emptied her glass and waved to the waiter, completely in charge.

'See? See the shit has a function? It fills up the hole!'

Ayane shook her head in pretend disbelief. The hairs of her smooth bob bounced playfully like in a L'Oréal-advert. I loved her. She was worth it.

Raf smiled at me as he came running up the steps, dripping, goggles on his head. He'd done his fifty pre-lunch lengths and was visibly chuffed with his effort. He held both arms up in the air like an Olympic champion.

Tamako and I were sitting at the table on the porch, surrounded by colourful sheets of textile, scissors and pots of glue; we were in the process of making our very own kite. Takuya was ecstatically pattering around on the terrace. 'Oh, for goodness sake.' Ayane gave the gate at the top of the stairs an angry kick with her bare foot. It clicked shut. 'There's a reason for this thing, you know.' She looked exhausted. 'Sorry,' Raf said in a little voice. Ayane pulled her son towards her. 'Once you have kids this becomes second nature, that's all.' I looked up from my handy work. 'Here's the thing, though, Ayanne: Raf and I *haven't got* kids. 'Em,' Raf tried with a schoolmaster's warning look in my direction, but the dance had started. I knew I should let it go, but I took a nasty pleasure in stirring up the smouldering flame.

Things were never just what they were. Couples in love experienced the world as an inviting vat of opportunities. In a tense relationship it was hard to focus on anything but the shortcomings of the other. Most people wouldn't dream of telling off a visitor for breaking their favourite wine decanter but might go ballistic if their nearest did just that. One tended to laugh with more conviction at mediocre jokes told by one's boss then by one's husband. With a troubled mind not even Fawlty Towers was funny.

For years Raf had been able to derive my moods from the stages of my menstrual cycles. Like a skilled sailor he knew which cliffs to avoid, his compass fine-tuned, set to navigate around my moods. Tricky matters were best tackled in the early stages of a new cycle, when everything was still light and filled with new hope. In relationships or friendship, one was never in neutral mode. Or in Ayane's words: 'There's always an agenda, Em. Always.'

Takuya was teething and kept his parents awake at night. During the day Ayane and Luc took it in turns to catch up on some sleep. Luc seemed to seize that opportunity a bit more often than his wife. It was a sensitive point. The fact that Raf and I, the childfree couple, took little trips out, did not exactly make things easier. We felt it was key to give them some space as a family, a bit of privacy, their parenting challenges being enough on display as it was. I'm not sure Ayane quite saw it like that.

'Oh, for God's sake, Emma, change the record, will you?'

'Why? Haven't heard you complain about our baby-sitting skills the past few days though, despite them not being part of our second nature.'

Tamako made big eyes at me, then at her mum. I needed to calm down.

'Fuck you, Emma.' Ayane grabbed hold of her son and clutched him in her arms as she whizzed past me hissing: 'That's too low even for you.'

'Oh, really? Even for me, is it? But lashing out at us in that passive aggressive way of yours is not, I suppose?'

'Come on, Tamako, we're going for a little lie down.'

'But mummy, I need to finish my kite. Isn't that right, aunty Em?'

'Of course, babe.' I gave her a warm look. *We* were happy. Her mother was trying to disrupt that. 'There's plenty of time for that later, darling, come along.' In his mother's arms Takuya was starting to whimper. 'Tamako! Here. Right now.' It was a tone that did not allow space for opposition. Ayane seldom raised her voice at the children. Tamako glided off her chair and ran to her mother, she looked confused. A big tear drop ran down her cheek. Just like her mother she was able to cry without a sound. The three of them disappeared towards the bedroom.

'Luc will laugh,' I said triumphantly but the irony was lost on my husband.

'How do you mean?'

'He did not sleep a wink last night. Neither of them did, actually.'

'Jesus, Em, was this really necessary?'

'Now we shall have it! I was bloody defending you.'

'I didn't need defending. Can't you see she is worn out? Besides she was right about the gate.'

'This was hardly about the gate, Raf.'

'Exactly.'

'What *exactly*?'

'Tell me, are you in need of another conflict-fix or what?'

'Don't be pathetic. Thanks, by the way, you're a picture of loyalty.'

'Loyalty? That's a good one coming from you.'

'Meaning?'

'Swallowing those self-righteous sentiments of yours for once would have been more loyal. Can't you see how they're both dying for some proper down time? How they gaze at us in envy every time we're off for a siesta or another evening stroll in the moonlight?'

'Fuck! Fat romance!' By now I was screaming at him as I was wildly gesticulating at my friend's bedroom. 'Those two sleepwalkers in there know damn well that I would give anything, literally anything, to spend hours on end tending to my wailing, puking, teething baby instead of...'

'Go on, finish your sentence, instead of faking romance in the moonlight with me?'

'Shit, Raf, but you know this, right?'

'What? That I'm a consolation prize? That spending a childless life with me feels more like a life sentence?' Raf grabbed his sweater from the chair. Without giving me another look he walked up to the baby gate, opened it, carefully closed it and walked down the stairs.

Here we go again, I thought. 'Raf? Where are you going? Come on, *Rafke*, don't do this, I did not mean it like that. You know what I'm like, right? Raf!' With straightened back, his head held high, Raf walked out of the front garden and in the direction of the Playa Isuledda. I knew there was no point in following him.

It was dark in Luc and Ayane's bedroom, apart from the glow of the night light in the corner by the settee on which Luc was stretched out. He looked wide awake. As he turned his head towards the open door I could faintly detect a wink. Tamako was sitting on a cushion at the low table by his side. She was organising her quartet cards in little heaps but sprang to her feet when she saw me come in. 'Auntie Em?' Luc held his index finger to his lips. 'Shhhh,' he whispered. Ayane and her son were sprawled out on the big bed. They looked fast asleep. That was quick. My friend was lying on her tummy in her pants. Her body rose and fell gently, almost imperceptibly. The straight locks of her bob covered the side of her face, fanning onto the pillow; a pose for a painting.

Takuya had thrown his little arms above his sweaty head, his legs too were wide apart. He formed an overwhelmingly cuddle-able, softly buzzing little X. Luc got up and walked towards me. He put his arm over my shoulder and whispered: 'Why don't you have a lie down on the sofa, I'm taking Tamako for a swim. Those two won't rest in peace for much longer, believe me.' He nodded towards the bed. 'Soon the beast will be hungry. Or in pain. Or both.'

'No, Luc, it's fine, later on I will...'

'I reckon you should join these two when they wake up, talk things through.'

'Did she tell you?' Luc nodded. For a moment it looked as though we had woken up Takuya. He made plaintive noises as he rocked his head back and forth. 'Oops.' But Luc just continued to talk in my ear, sotto voce. 'God, it's no big deal, Em, she loves you to bits.'

'Shit, Luc, I seem to make a mess of everything. Now Raf's on the run as well.'

'You're kidding? Oh, dear, those Hollanders,' he chuckled and turned to his daughter as he held out his hand. 'Shall we go snorkelling, *Tammeke*?'

As always, I felt his Flemish take on the girl's name was much like its Japanese original. Perhaps Flemish had a Japanese quality. Tamako obediently switched off the light and walked towards her dad. She pulled a face but nonetheless took his hand. There would be no kite flying today, so much was clear. Luc softly pulled the door behind them.

Ayane's breathing was slow and incredibly deep. This was not just something that happened when she slept. A fervent yogini, my dancer friend had astonishing control of her breathing. She claimed that yoga 'informed' her dancing, made it wiser and more layered. After all, the *vinyassa*, one of Astanga yoga's main principles, was about breathing and movement. Not only did it claim to make the body lighter and suppler, it was also said to strengthen it and provide it with purpose and inner fire. I would have signed up for that, if it hadn't been for my lack of belief and motivation. When I had taken it up a few years ago it had been purely with the view to giving birth naturally.

There was something exhilarating about this secret spying on my sleeping friend. I bent over the bed. Ayane's mouth was slightly open, the crowns of her small, regular bottom teeth were visible. On her top lip minuscule beads of sweat were gathering. Her hand, which was resting on the pillow, made a few involuntary jerks. The black varnish on her nails was starting to peel away. Before setting off we'd been to the salon together and had had our nails done in the same colour. Unlike Ayane, I made a point of keeping mine pristine and regularly touched them up. It was what she liked to rub in, quasi joking, that even on holiday she didn't find the time to 'fiddle around with her body'. A thinly disguised insinuation that would hurt me more than she would ever know, for all this body-fiddling was nothing if not a substitute for meaningful tamperings, a truth I for one did not need convincing of. Changing shitty nappies and terrified vigils at a struggling baby's bed side, were, for me too, so much more part of veritable, dignified womanhood.

What was going on in that stubborn, arty head of hers? I often wondered about those closest to me: who in fact were they and how did they really see me? Ayane, Raf, Luc? At times I felt I caught a glimpse, at others I hadn't the faintest idea. Most of the time my own words and actions made utter sense and I knew I wasn't alone in that. What drove me was my first, most instinctive reflex. Then doubt would creep in. Self-examination. Repentance. Was that a weakness or a strength? Was it coincidence that I had chased away both my lover and best friend in less than an hour?

I carefully tip toed to the other side of the bed to study my godson. His pouting lips made funny little twitches, as though there was a fly on his nose, irritating him. Ayane was very generous with her children, she loved that I loved them, she loved sharing them with me. I knew plenty of women who claimed their kids to such a degree that any sign of interest in their offspring was met with a level of suspicion, especially if the attention provider happened to be a poor unwanted childless loser; I suspected they had alarm systems in their prams. I loved my friend's children equally, yet my affection for Takuya somehow felt different, weightier, as though I was permanently aware of the importance of the responsibility his parents had entrusted me with. I kept on applying for the job I'd already bagged.

Takuya opened his eyes. A myriad of expressions lit up his little face: fear, irritation, joy. Finally, he opted for a broad smile as he started to shriek, at the top of his voice, while he raised his arms towards me.
'Hey? Hello my boy! Who's awake then? My little Takki-takki-tee? Yes?' I spoke softly but it only seemed to provoke more energetic squealing. 'Shhh, *stillekes* man, mummy's asleep. Can auntie Em come and lie next to you, bibsee? Yes? You like this, huh?'
I lay down on the bed next to Takuya. He wriggled himself close up to me and started to screech with delight, his feisty hands were flapping on either side of my face. He started to squeeze my cheeks with force. 'Hey, take it easy, little man.'
There was movement from the other side of the bed. A throat was being cleared. At any other time, there would be a 'Hey, gorgeous'. But this was not any other time and things weren't what they were.

'Aya?' My friend did not reply. I pulled myself up and leaned on one elbow. Ayane's eyes were closed but she was clearly awake, she licked her dry lips. Takuya was using me as a climbing frame.
'Aya,' I said. 'I'm sorry.' She sighed and opened her eyes, fixing them, void of expression, on a point near my chin, as if I were a hologram. Was she buying to time to consider her response? Was she so exhausted that

sighing was all she could do? Did she regret her invitation and was she fed up with my presence? Takuya was bored with his climbing frame and started to pull at my hair with mean little tugs.

'Auch, Ta-ak!'

'Takuya! Stop that.' Ayane grabbed her son and firmly dumped him on his bottom in between the two of us. She should have known: the *Padmasana* was the most favourable *Asana* to enable ultra-deep breathing. With maximum lung capacity Takuya started to howl. It was impressive to behold such a small, compact human bundle surrender to such an intense performance; razor-sharp, sand bursting with dramatic awareness. Inadvertently my mouth curled into the beginning of a smile, which, from a pedagogical point of view, I tried to fight. From the corner of my eye I saw my friend do the same. When we could no longer hold it together and almost simultaneously burst into laughter, our little man fell silent. This clearly wasn't the reaction he was expecting from his audience and with our laughing faces as a mirror and being the accomplished actor he was, he continued his chameleon act and started to chuckle as though his life depended on it.

When Ayane looked at me her face had turned serious again. For the time being we had laughed enough. 'Listen, Emma, I know I have been rather touchy, the last few days. But you must also know I'm not always finding it easy to see how you and Raf have all this carefree time together.'

'Ha. That's a good one.'

'No, of course you wouldn't see it like that, why would you? I know very well there are still tensions and so on. But...'

'But what?' I needed to snap out of this gooey victim part. I was so fed up with my own long-suffering voice, its flat, colourless melody. She was right. We did sometimes enjoy our time together, Raf and I, despite everything. The long beach walks, the siestas. We'd had had better sex here than we'd been having for months. But what did that mean? According to Raf I was always up for a shag, war or not. In that respect he thought of the two I was probably the bigger macho, the one for whom a loving relationship was not necessarily a condition for great sex. But now I had ruined that too.

'But I've just about had it with that oversensitivity of yours. Ok, you don't have children and I think that is so unfair and awful and hard for you both. But, Em. Look at me!' Now it was me who was ruining my perfect nails. With masochistic pleasure I pulled at the shiny black texture that was covering the nail of my ring finger, the entire coat came off. I looked up.

'Move on!'

I nodded while I looked at my friend, meekly. 'I hear you.'

'Ok, but do it, Emma. Stop going on about it, stop hearing me, Just...*assume*.'

'What?'

'*Assume*, take responsibility, do something with it, take stock, move on, what do I know? *Assume*. That's how they say it in French anyway. Oh, whatever. Come here, you hysterical woman, I love you so, do you realise that? Do you? No, seriously?'

I fell into her arms like a child. I was not going to cry, definitely not, no more corny, self-pitying blur. But the tears were already running over my cheeks.

'I thought you regretted having me here.'

'You bet! I did!' She patted me on the back, mildly, yet forcefully, as though I was in need of a burp.

'I did today, oh *Emmetje*, *Emmetje*. It's alright, come here, my stubborn little noodle.' Ayane rocked me in her arms. 'Silly little loser, come here, it's ok.'

'It's not!' This was pathetic, snot was running down my nose. 'It's not ok, nothing is.'

Takuya was clapping his hands excitedly and made endearing little clucking noises that seemed to come from deep down in his throat. It was our turn to perform.

Raf and Luc were out on the terrace playing a game of chess as I walked towards them with Takuya on my arm. Raf had his back towards me. Tamako was sitting next to her dad, behind a big sheet of paper. Our kite materials had been moved to the far side of the table. She looked at me and pulled a face. Luc gave me a fat wink. 'Ça va?'

'Yes, ça va. You guys too ?' Against the odds I was hoping Raf would turn around to face me and break the ice with a joke or a trivial remark. But his angry back did not look very forgiving.

'Sure we are, I'm flooring that husband of yours, as per usual.' Raf gave no comment. That would mean allowing me into their private bubble. My stomach shrivelled. Not that again. Not the sulking. Not now. Don't go shutting me out, not here on holiday. For God's sake make an effort man, we're not on our own here. I smiled at my godson. 'Where's big sis?' I had a lump in my throat. 'Shall we go and look what she's drawing, bear? What do you say?' Tamako shielded her drawing with her arm. 'It's not finished yet.' I knew it wasn't just our interrupted craft session she had the hump about; she was also peeved about the attention I was giving her brother.

'Are we going to draw something ourselves then?' I climbed onto the bench next to Raf and plonked Takuya in his thick nappy in between us.

'Check mate, mister Bakker.' Luc held his hand in the air, inviting a *high five*. He was the only one keeping the spark. 'Well done.' Raf slapped Luc's hand and glided off the bench without looking at me. He got up, stretched and continued to talk to Luc alone. 'I'm going for a dip. Care to join me?'

'Why not? You ok here for a bit, love, with the kiddies?' Luc squeezed my shoulder. I appreciated he was trying to comfort me but it only made me more melancholic. 'Course I am.'

Tamako shifted her arm and pushed her drawing over to the one I had started with her brother. 'Wow. Is that me in the blue bikini?' She nodded shyly. 'D'you think you could you add your mummy in her new shoes?' I handed her back the drawing. She obliged straight away and began to scribble. It felt somehow different, this dispute. More absolute. More final. Should I have bitten my tongue? Should I have been more patient, milder? I pressed my face into Takuya's sweaty crown, he purred. As I was quietly crying, my lamenting was soaked up by my godson's soft baby-hair, which faintly smelt of cinnamon.

Ayane took a sip of her rosé and patted her face with a piece of kitchen towel. It was still very warm outside, the midnight air felt sticky and oppressive. 'I think it was a bloody courageous initiative. Now that it has caught on everyone seems to think its success was predictable but for the same token it could have flopped, right?' She looked from me to Luc. 'If it really were such an obvious formula then why did nobody think of it before? You can say what you like Luc, but she's got balls that Australian lady.' My friend was trying hard to make the atmosphere seem natural and light but both Raf and I ignored the bait of her animated conversation. Only Luc was willing to offer a lukewarm response. 'You could say that, I suppose.' Ayane's husband smiled unconvincingly while he started to clear the table, making sure to avoid eye contact with me or Raf. In the Autumn Ayane would be dancing in her very own solo production. She had been shortlisted for the latest edition of *Coupe Maison*, an experimental programme of *Flanders Ballet* in which promising dancers were given the opportunity to choreograph their own work. It proved to be a popular formula and the majority of the performances sold out in no time. Amongst the dancers too there was huge excitement about the initiative. It was not every day that they were offered a platform to show what they were made of, away from the preformed concepts and the safety nets of established directors and choreographers. Ayane tended to talk about her upcoming challenge when she'd had a bit too much to drink. 'Oh, never mind. If no one is listening I'm off for a little plunge.'

'You *what*? You want to go swimming? Now?' Luc looked at his wife in disbelief. 'For heaven's sake don't be such a wimp. There are lights by the pool, aren't there? I promise I won't drown. Just fancy a little cool-off dip before bed, that's all.' She had already opened the gate and was walking down the stairs, taking off her T-shirt. 'Aya!' Luc looked over his shoulder at the two of us in pretend panic. I smiled. Raf did not. Raf remained stone faced. He was sitting opposite me, rigid, hands curled around his beer as if he were clutching a comforting mug of glühwein après-ski. Luc had switched on the lights to the pool, he was following his wife down. Ayane was standing next to the pool, completely naked, in the full glare of the lights. She made a clumsy little bow. 'And now, ladies and gentlemen, the moment you have all been waiting for: Ayane Watanabe in her very own composition *Flow, water, flow;* a daring, inspiring, but above all, stark bollock naked water ballet!' And with that she dived into the pool. It was a most elegant performance. She was Poseidon's wife Amphitrite, the Greek goddess of the ocean. She was Ariel, the divine little mermaid, playing to her doting audience on the shore. Luc was sitting on the edge of the pool with his legs in the water, he was doubled over, he had the giggles. I looked at Raf. 'Look at them.' He turned to me and spoke in a tone cold as ice. 'Can we go for a little walk, Emma? There's something I'd like to discuss with you.' My guts were wriggling.

We walked down the narrow dune path behind one another. Who was making up the choreography for this dance? A few days ago, we had walked here side by side, holding hands. Had that been sincerely idyllic or one of the many attempts to bridge the gap with a romantic cliché? I didn't know where trying had become forcing. Already we looked like a parody of ourselves. Nothing seemed straight forward anymore, least of all my feelings. Suddenly that became the scariest thing of all: how was I to know what I wanted? What was I entitled to and what was realistic? Wanting was endless but I seemed to have lost the ability to assess the foundation of my needs. I had become so skilled at denial. Denial had become so much second nature.

'Emma?' Raf was standing right in front of me, moonlit and statuesque, a pained look on his face, the sigh of the sea put in for good measure, emphasising finality. I was hoping for an original script. Suddenly he was a complete stranger.

'What?'

'Shall we sit down here?'

'Sure.'

From our rugged dune seats, we looked out over the silvery water deck; the ultimate setting for a weighty scene: the epilogue?

'Emma, I have made a decision.' A lousy script, as it turned out.

'I know.' I was curious to learn what else would roll from my tongue. I was in free fall.

'What do you mean?'

The words came to me as in a déjà vu, they were there at the forefront of my brain, fully formed, all I had to do was open my mouth. 'Your decision. I won't fight it. Me too, I want it to stop.' What had I just said?

'Do you mean that?'

'Yes. We're done. This thing has run its course. Is that what you feel too?'

'Yes. Something like that.' Raf turned towards me and took my hand.

'Em, this is ok, right? This is good, is it not? Before we cause each other any more damage?'

I pulled my hand away from his. 'What is it? Are you hesitating? Had you expected more resistance?' There it was: an unexpected cruel turn of my character, she was not so one-dimensional after all.

'Yes, actually. Or, no, perhaps not, I'm not sure. I'm not sure what I expected. It's just, I can't do this anymore, you see, I can't do this and be true to myself at the same time, to my own expectations. It kills me.'

'What does?'

'The fact that we no longer bring out the best in each other.'

'Quiet. We don't.' Our Joni Mitchells song. Many moons ago we had sung it in one voice, under a starry sky at Stokes Bay, surrounded by kangaroos. *All I really want our love to do is to bring out the best in me and in you. I want to be the one that you want to see. I wanna have fun, I wanna shine like the sun.* I no longer shone like the sun. When had I become so icy? Had it been wriggling there all long, under the skin, ready to break out, this awareness, this death-wish for a suffocating pact?

'Listen, Emma, I don't regret what we've had. I do regret things have turned out this way but I guess...'

I wanted him to stop talking. I wanted to put him on *silent*, as I did with my mobile during a meeting. I wanted to run away. Be alone with my thoughts. Get in touch with this me I did not recognise.

'Raf, stop. Not now, please. I'm going back to the house. I just want to be by myself for a bit, ok?'

'But of course it is. I want to get this right, Emma, I want to do my best the rest of this week, with our friends, you know?' His reasonableness was what irritated me most. He was a fake, why had I not seen that? A cardboard cut-out. *I don't regret us.* We're all winners here. Bloody Dutch liberal-anything-goes-crap.

'Yes.' I got up and walked down the dune path with rubbery legs. When I reached the house, the only lights on were at the terrace where Luc was sitting at the table with his laptop and a pot of coffee.

'That's quick.'

'Yes. Aya's gone to bed?'

'What do you think? She collapsed like a sack of potatoes after her drunken water ballet.' He shook his head, endeared and switched off his laptop. I studied my best friend's husband's face. There were bags under his eyes and on his bottom lip a cold sore was starting to come out. What would it be like to be married to him?

Luc was not exactly an attractive man but he had something about him. Would I argue with him all the time too and finally call it a day and wish him luck? Or would he be able to tame me, to calm me down? It was all so random. If I hadn't bumped into that old friend of mine, the year after I graduated from drama school and hadn't become so intrigued with her passion for jewellery design, I would probably not have signed up for that silversmith course in Ireland and I wouldn't have met Sean and therefore never have visited Sydney when I did. Without New-Zealand-Tammy I would not have explored the rest of Kangaroo Island, but most likely have returned to Adelaide to celebrate New Year. One day earlier in Adelaide and I would not have met Raf. Perhaps another man. I would have had a different life with different set-backs and successes. With different expectations, different fears, different delights. *Different how?*

Luc folded down the screen of his laptop. I was still standing by his chair. He looked up.

'You ok, Em?'

'No.' I closed my eyes. I would have liked to have felt something.

'Is there anything I can get you? Coffee, a nice cold coke, perhaps or a night cap? Luc got up and rubbed his hands over my upper arms as if to stimulate the blood flow there. I looked into his tired eyes.

'A pint. A nice cold pint, that's what I want.'

'Coming up, *madammeke*.' Luc hurried to the kitchen and returned almost immediately with a beer and a bottle opener. He opened the bottle, poured me my beer and himself a cup of lukewarm coffee. He rummaged in the biscuit tin. 'Bicky?' I smiled. Luc would never have a coffee without dunking *speculaas*-bisuits into it. Luc made coffee to go with *speculaas*, not the other way round, he'd brought his own supply from home.

'It's over, Luc. Raf and I are splitting up.'

'Of course you're not. It's what it feels like now. You're going through a difficult episode, that's all.'

'Luc?' I leaned towards him and held his eyes. 'It is finished. Done. *Schluss*. Raf wants it, I want it. At least I think that's what I thought a few minutes ago. The penny hasn't quite dropped yet. God, this is so weird.'

'Shit, Emma. I can hardly believe that. What happened? You've been for a walk, right?

'Raf told me he had made a decision. I replied I knew and that I was ok about it, that I felt the same in fact. Then he had a sort of surprised reaction, hardly believing that I took it so well, I guess that kind of gave him second thoughts, something like that anyway. But we both agreed this was staring us in the face. Then we, I...'

'What?'

'Then I walked back.'

'That's it?'

I nodded. I looked at myself through Luc's eyes. *Drama queen. Before long they'll fall into each other's arms again.* Or not? *At last. About time too.* Did it matter how other people saw you? Whether they believed in our causes or in us?

'You don't decide things like that on impulse, Em. You two have been through far too much for that.'

'Exactly. Which is why you can hardly call this an impulse. Maybe we've got too much baggage. I can't say I'm utterly devastated. As a matter of fact, I feel very little.'

'You're in shock.'

'No. Definitely not that.'

'Then what?'

'Indifference.'

'No way.'

'Maybe that's too strong. But a form of relief, for sure.' Luc kept staring at me. In the end he started to stir his cold coffee. 'Would you like to sleep in our bed tonight?'

Ayane was snoring loudly. For the second time that day I slid into bed next to my friend. She did a silly half twist, flopping a limp arm over me. I caught a whiff of her sour wine-breath as she mumbled something vague about pool lights.

I liberated myself, tucked the arm beside her body. 'Shhhh, go to sleep.' I softly stroked her sweaty crown. She gave one super long snore and all went quiet.

The room was no longer pitch black. On the ceiling the moonlight was casting frivolous patterns to the rhythm of the blowing curtains in the night breeze. From the terrace came the faint sound of male voices.

I replayed our conversation in the dunes. *I've made a decision.* He had sounded so sure. How long had this been fermenting? My reaction to the gate couldn't have been more than the last straw. Two days ago, we had made love so tenderly and laughed like teenagers when Raf's leg had gone into a cramp when he was about to orgasm. Did that not mean anything? Had our joy been insincere? Or did none of this weigh up against the ferocity of our clashes? Were we too much in the habit of turning ourselves inside out, against the odds, like characters in a play, in the hope of embarking on some new resource? I wasn't sure. I was waiting for notes from my director. An actor could feed off everything. There isn't an emotion that can't be used on set or on stage, in search of the truth of a performance. When was enough enough? When is a painting finished, a poem or a story? When is something over? When do we stop trying? I could have endured a few more pregnancies.

Me too, I want it to stop. This thing has run its course. A line from a soap. Had I tried to top his grim determination in order not to lose face or was I softening the blow of his words with my own tough reply? Without a script an escalating dispute is for the most part bluff. Barking. Letting off steam. Passing on the pain. *I want you to hurt like I do,* as Randy Newman would have it. But there were things we could not take back. Our break-up dialogue would forever be hanging over the dunes of Playa Isuledda. Or would that too evaporate? Was this perhaps not our real ending? This was how it always went. Whenever I felt Raf genuinely started to doubt us, my panic would set in and all of a sudden, I'd be up for another round. When I myself was tempted by a better life, away from our coupledom, I wanted to be able to flee in one swift, flamboyant move, only to realise that took an awful lot of guts. In my internal monologues that dilemma had become crucial: which one of us would one day harvest that kind of courage? It had turned out to be Raf and that was that. What I felt now was not panic but something altogether more hollow, not unlike the sluggish emptiness post miscarriage. A sedated pinching to the core accompanied by a sense of relief: at least it had happened. Permeated by the irreversibility of its trauma, the body seemed to restore its calm by surrendering. *I don't regret what we've had*. As it started to settle, it sounded less pathetic. I didn't regret us either. Wasn't that a good thing? Just as I didn't regret my miscarriages for that would feel like a betrayal of my unborn children. At least I had entered the club, I knew what it felt like to expect. In my mind it would have been worse not to have become a mother without ever having been pregnant. Why was that? Was leaving Raf a betrayal of the family we might have become? People seldom owned up to their regrets, as though that somehow spoiled their stories or made them less credible. What was the point in suffering if not to make one's journey feel less random? Do we delude ourselves with the belief that pain has a function? *What doesn't kill you makes you stronger.* Bullshit. We had nothing to show for our struggles, instead they had worn us out. It was better to face that.

I pulled the sheet over my face, wiping away the tears. I was worn out. Enough. We were both in need of a new beginning and if we were lucky, one day our history would no longer contaminate our friendship. Luc would sleep on the settee in the sitting room tonight. He'd promised to have a quick chat with Raf. For now, I needed some time alone. Tomorrow I would allow myself to send Joris a text. I would also try to find a way to make the most of this last trip with Raf. With the help of our friends we would be able to round off this holiday with minimum upset.

I had no idea that would no longer be possible.

Part 4

I woke up in an empty bed. The terrace was on the wrong side. Then I remembered. The shock for which I braced myself did not come. Instead, a vague feeling of unease caused my stomach to contract as if I was about to take on a job I dreaded. I wanted to fast forward the days and months ahead, to escape the raw sharpness of this split. I longed to be alone. I felt an overwhelming need to decode what was happening, away from the added pressure of being amongst friends. Away from aunty Em and all the other Ems I had ceased to be.

From the terrace came the cheerful sounds of morning. Chirpy voices and the clattering of cutlery. 'Takú, don't!' Tamako's irritated voice was followed by Luc's mediating tone as he tried to distract his daughter. 'Oh, leave him, sis, he's not breaking it, is he? Why don't you come and sit with me? No?' *Tammeke* was the apple of his eye, his first born, his wife's clone. Ayane would know by now why Luc had slept on the couch and I had ended up sharing her bed. She would not be all that surprised. Just as I was wondering if Raf was up, I heard his voice. 'Morning, guys.' Ayane gave a reply I could not hear. 'Amazingly well, actually.' Muffled laughter. So, he had slept well, the thought stabbed me. *Fast forward.* The bedroom door slid open, Tamako carefully, tentatively popped her head through. 'Hey there, hamster, you've come to join me?' She rushed towards the bed, the sticky patter of her bare feet thudding the stone floor. I held up the sheet. 'Come in, tucky, tucky.' Tamako curled her warm body around mine. I folded her into my arms and waited for her cross-examination.
'Auntie Em?'
'Tamako?'
'Why did you sleep in my mummy's bed?' Nothing escaped her. Once again, I tried out a child friendly version of my relationship tumult. At least I would not have to do that for much longer. I sighed and stroked her gentle little head. The words came with surprising ease.
'Don't worry, *boopie*, auntie Em and uncle Raf have had a bit of a quarrel, that's all.'
'Why? Don't you like uncle Raf anymore?'
'Of course I do.'
'Does uncle Raf not like *you* anymore?'
'I'm sure he does. It's just...' Just what? Was it fair to fob her off with the juvenile equivalent of crap phrases about *letting go* and no being blame? She was a cool, bright kid, on holiday with everyone who was dear to her and our spat was not part of the deal.

96

'It's just, we no longer want to share everything.'

'Like a house and stuff?'

'Exactly.'

'Are you getting divorced?' It was clearly something she knew.

'Perhaps', I said lightly. 'But we'll always be friends, uncle Raf and I, that's for sure.' The girl nodded in silence. Even a seven-year-old felt the inevitability. That it would be best no longer to share houses and stuff.

'Two more days and we're back in rainy homeland.' Luc undid Takuya's bib, lifted him out of the high chair and onto his lap. I studied my peanut butter sandwich with huge interest. When he looked up and saw nobody reacting he mumbled: 'Sorry'.

Raf was the first one to burst into laughter. Then I did. Takuya looked from one to the other. He clapped his hands and began to screech the way only he could, at the top of his voice. Ayane looked at her boy in amusement. 'What do you think you're doing, you clown? Hey? What's so funny?' When Ayane and Luc joined in with the giggles, their son's excitement peaked; blaring like an exotic bird caught in a net, his deafening little falsetto bellowed across the bay. Tamako's serious face seemed set, but looking around the table she too finally cracked. When we all fell silent and Takuya indulged in his last showy hic-ups, Raf said: 'Listen guys, I don't want the atmosphere to get all heavy and for us to pussy foot around each other here in a depressed sort of fashion, ok? Em and I will be fine. Right?' He looked at me. I nodded. Raf was right and he should have left it at that but he went on to milk his patronising view point. 'Perhaps it's for the best things were decided here, in this magical setting.' He made a wide arm gesture towards the sea, as if he were Jesus of Nazareth. 'I'm sure it's no coincidence, albeit little consolation and bad timing indeed, Aya. We are truly sorry about that.' Jesus looked at me. 'Aren't we, Emma?' He almost sounded on a high. I was still nodding like a simpleton, a velvety long eared toy dog in the back of the car. I hated that he had framed it and claimed it. He was being the archetypal liberal Dutch man, smooth and logical. *The sky is the limit. Let's embrace life in all its whimsical splendour. Every knock-back is part of this glorious adventure called life, right guys?* Perhaps I felt embarrassed at the phoney public display. Perhaps I finally allowed myself to look at him without forgiving glasses. This morning I had sent Joris a text message, after Tamako had sneaked out of the bed. 'Holiday disaster. Proper Shriver-script. Hope you're having a better time.' I regretted it straight away. Joris was spending the second month of the school holidays at his parents' house in the Dordogne together with his kids. He had not yet replied. 'Nonsense.' Ayane coolly wiped her mouth with her serviette. 'These aren't exactly things one can plan.' The tip of the napkin brushed the corner of her eye. She sniffed and got up to go to the kitchen. 'Will you bring in your plate, honey?' Tamako got up, took her little plate and followed her mum into the kitchen. My loyal friend was upset. All this time she had genuinely hoped we would make it. Again, I asked myself if this was pure altruism. After all, befriended couples splitting up, be it kicking and screaming or signing a sensible peace treaty, eroded the fairy tale.

All kitted out, we headed for the beach. Tamako was dragging her feet, trotting in between me and Ayane. She was struggling with her flip-flops but had stubbornly refused to wear her sandals and had been equally insistent on transporting our massive inflatable beach ball. She held it tightly under her arm, locked in an uncomfortable grip. She had tried to carry it in front of her, but had not been able to see where she was going. I was pushing the pram in which Takuya was dosing under his sunhat. By the time we found our spot on the playa Isuledda, he would be fast asleep. Ayane would drape a towel over the pram and revel in some precious time to herself, a chance to catch up with *Dance Magazine*, before the beast would rattle its cage again.

The men walked ahead. Luc was carrying the rucksack and a large parasol. His calves were still bright red. In the first days of the holiday he had been badly burnt. The skin on his shoulders had started to peel, big flaps of dried skin were coming away. Raf, who was towering beside him, looked like a native. His arms and legs had a uniform walnut colour, his neck and shoulders were darker still. He held a beach bag stuffed with snorkels, spades, shapes, towels, a canvas and our entire arsenal of sunscreens: from a mild fifteen for those of us with a seasoned tan all the way up to the plaster sealant of sunscreen fifty, for noses, birth marks, bald patches and the baby.

It was eleven and the sun was already merciless. The beach was strewn with for the most part Italian tourists. Small groups of teenagers were making their way towards the cafeteria, carrying huge vintage ghetto blasters on their frail shoulders. Parents with children behind wind shields, industrious mothers on little fold up seats busy with Tupperware pots and cool boxes. Young girls fooling around in the surf; carefree, supple bodies with tanned legs and alert little breasts, underneath two bits of triangular cloth and some string, their very first bikinis.

We walked to the furthest part of the beach, which was less crowded. Towards the end was a narrow band of rocks with shallow pools of water one could easily wade through to reach deeper sea inlets which were perfect for snorkelling. We started to unpack. Luc put up the parasol and spread the canvas. He found a cool spot for the rucksack with our provisions. Ayane put out some towels. Raf unloaded his beach bag and organised everything neatly on the canvas. I found a bottle of sunscreen twenty-five and started on Tamako, who was dosing off against the beach ball, her flip-flops were lying in the sand beside her. We had perfected this routine. After all, this was something Ayane had been clear about from day one: 'In and around the house as well as on the beach, with kids the secret is organisation. Once you've established a routine, you're safe and able to embrace your own enjoyment. Pure logic, no?' Raf and I had joked about it during our siesta a few days earlier: 'Jesus, one tends to forget what a luxury that is: walking to the beach in swimming trunks, towel over shoulder, book in hand, flop down in sand, nap, swim, read.' I had laughed and agreed.

Raf and Luc had gone snorkelling. For a while I had entertained Tamako with a beach ball contest by the water's edge but the wind had started to make it difficult and before long she had wanted to return to her mummy under the parasol and curl up next to her in the shade. Now she was lying on a towel clutching her rabbit. She was humming and chewing a dry biscuit, a picture of peace. Ayane, who had discarded her *Dance Magazine*, was watching me through drooping eyes. I was applying sunscreen to my arms and legs. My tan was as deep as Raf's. 'Can you do my back, Aya?'
'Course hon, hand me that.' She stooped on to her knees, took the bottle from me and squirted cream on her hands. Sitting behind me she started to generously massage my back, it felt good.
'Mmm. Nice.'
'How are you feeling? Or is that an impossible question?'
'It is a bit. I'm not sure, mixed. Groggy. Sad too. But then again, also somewhat...'
'Relieved?'
'I wouldn't go as far as that. But slightly hopeful, I guess. As if there's a crack that will allow all the shit, all the puss to escape. Something like that, anyway. Do you know what I mean?'
'I guess so.' Ayane kneaded my neck.
'As if the vicious circle is broken and we're actually heading somewhere, we're no longer perpetually chasing our tails. I don't know. To be honest, it feels different from one moment to the next.'
'That's not surprising. Do you think this is it, that it's real, this time?'

Ayane rubbed the remainder of the cream over her own arms. I turned around to face her and sat with my back towards the sun.

'I think so, yes. Yes, I think so.' Ayane nodded. 'That's what it feels like to me too.'

I tried to smile and kept looking at her, quietly, while the tears began to flow. 'It's OK *Emmetje*, come here...hug?' We held each other tightly. 'O shit, all this shit carry-on,' I sighed. Ayane let go of me and wiped away her own tears. She felt for me, *with* me. This was what *com-passion* meant. Feeling someone else's pain. Was I able to do that? How could I have doubted her integrity? For a moment I wanted to confess to her about the text message, but I was too frightened of her reaction.

'This is big, Em. It's normal to feel confused. It's bound to go up and down for quite a while. With good days and bad. I know it sounds a cliché, love. Perhaps Raf was right and there is a blessing in that it happened here and now, in this perfect setting.'

'Good grief, Aya, give me a break. That esoteric nonsense is wasted on me. Honestly, I have no time for his patronising crap.'

'I could see that.'

I slapped my thighs and looked up at Tamako. 'Tammeke?'

'Yes?'

'Are we going to open that shop of ours, or what?' The girl shot upright.

'Yes!' she cried out excitedly and straight away began to gather her shapes and shells. Faint murmurings could be heard from the pram.

'Do you want cucumber too, Emma, or just tomato?'

'You can do me both, ta.' Raf dished salad on to my paper plate. The two men had returned from their snorkel expedition like elated school boys. 'Long, elegant black and white fish, with delicate tails, honestly, you have to see this.'

'Like those aniseedy liquorish sweets, you know, the bi-coloured ones', Luc added to the description.

'What kind of sweets, daddy?'

'You've got her attention, Luc,' Ayane laughed, while she shoved another piece of peach in the baby's mouth; the juice was running down his chin. Seated on his bottom on the canvas, wearing nothing but his nappy, Takuya was covered in bits of food. With his little chubby hands, he was slapping his bare legs, as he screeched in delight. We took it in turns to feed him, we simply couldn't help ourselves, for both in posture and in rapturous response

Takuya reminded us of *Gust*, once Antwerp Zoo's most famous lowland-gorilla.

Back in the house everyone headed off for a siesta. Tamako wanted to share her mother's big bed. Luc, who had tucked in the baby, aimed for the shade of the back yard. He was reading 'King Leopold's Ghost', a gripping but tragic account of the Congolese suppression by our fellow-countrymen. He had not been able to put it down.

I too wanted to take a nap but was wondering how it would work in the room I shared with Raf. Fortunately, he beat me to it. 'Do you want to go for a sleep, Emma?' The past twenty-four hours I had become the full Emma again. Abbreviations, never mind how practical, were a form of intimacy.
'Yes, I wouldn't mind a little lie down, away from this heat.'
'Do you mind if I have a sleep too?'
'Of course not.'

Apart from the double bed, our room contained a single. Raf took off his sandals and pulled back the sheets. I went to lie on the big one. Unlike the past few days I kept on my t-shirt and shorts. It felt odd.
'I have the feeling it's even hotter than yesterday.'
'Yes, I think so too,' Raf replied. 'Slightly more humid. Luckily there's that bit of wind.' He turned his back to me to signal he wanted to sleep. It was a foreign language in which I was learning to converse. I was relieved it was possible for us to be together in this matter-of-fact way without the need to revisit our struggle. Suddenly New-Zealand-Tammy came to mind. *A marriage falls apart in stages.* Funny, I had forgotten all about that. When we met she had only just divorced. I had lent her a polite ear and had listened patiently to her tale of trial and error, it had all sounded very raw still. Here and there I had managed to interrupt her monologue with a fake empathetic question, but in the end, I could not relate to any of it. Until you experience your own, other people's insights rarely mean anything. I was hearing Tammy's words and had linked them to my own insubstantial life and love trajectory.

What did I know about the pitfalls of long relationships? To me it was quite simple: there was a click or there wasn't. In that case the magic had clearly run its course and you moved on. Simple as that. The twilight zone in between the two was nothing but self-delusion. Denial. Fear of the alternative. Lack of courage. This would never happen to me: kids or no kids, staying with someone for any other reason than love, respect and good sex: no way. 'It's a dance, Emma, back and forth and back and forth, until you can no longer move. After that you're not dancing for a while, I can tell you that much.' *Thet much*, it had sounded. How would she be doing now? She had to be in her sixties. I wondered if she would be dancing again. Raf's snoring mingled with the sound of the crickets. I closed my eyes. Perhaps I could find her on *Facebook*.

I woke up from an overheated sleep. I had dreamt I was on board a tiny sailboat but there was hardly any wind. I was just bobbing along on a colossal lake. Raf stood on the bank of the lake. He was waving his arms and shouting instructions, raging. But I couldn't hear him, he was too far away. His brother, who was sitting in the grass next to him, looked on and took photographs. At one point I got the giggles and that seemed to infuriate Raf even more. The more outrageous his gestures became, the more uncontrollably I laughed. When finally my boat capsized and I tried to swim to the shore, the coast started to drift away from me, further and further. In my dream I remained calm.
In real life Raf was still snoring. I looked at my watch, it was four o'clock. I had slept for almost two hours.

In the shower I re-lived my dream. I was not big on Freudian dream analyses, even if there was obviously a connection between day time worries and night time imagery. But who was to say which?
What was on the mind was bound to fester and a more symbolic version would sneak into dreams.

While I dried myself, I entertained my therapist's interpretation. *Is it possible, Emma, that the central theme of your dream is the breakdown in communications between you and Raf? A rhetorical question, of course. What do you think is happening? Could your uncontrollable laughter be about your deep need for things to remain light? Your need to remain in balance? Could it perhaps signal your belief in finding the strength to come out of this episode stronger? And what about your brother in law, who is standing by and making notes? Your husband's clan, perhaps, the opposition, who are coldly registering but already distancing themselves from your need? But you're not allowing it to impact, for you swim on, despite the retreating shore? In the face of your ordeal you feel calm, right? Does that not fill you with hope?*

I reapplied sunscreen. Before dinner we would probably all have another swim. It was actually the softest time of the day, still warm but no longer swelteringly hot. The sun was lower, a saturating fatigue came over us, soon we'd have our aperitif, someone would start cooking, the others would give the kids a quick bath and put them to bed or light the candles and lay the table. It would be time for grown up time, even if for me the enjoyment was less obvious now.

Naked it looked as if I was wearing a flesh coloured bikini, my body was evenly tanned and I enjoyed that. In fact, I thought I looked rather well, despite everything. *My limbs were sharp*, as Ayane would say it. I applied some mascara, combed my hair, tied it into a loose knot and put on perfume.
A summery, citrusy scent, *French Connection UK*, Raf's present from our London trip. A small melancholic wave. I heard him get up and walk out of the room. From the terrace the sound of Ayane's laughter.

Luc was in the back yard. Ayane was on the terrace with both her kids. Raf was helping Tamako put on her swimsuit.

'Here,' Ayane said while she handed me the baby. Takuya gave me a solemn smile. 'I'm just going to get into my bikini. You will join us, won't you?', my friend asked me on her way to the bathroom.

'You bet', I replied. 'I've already got mine on underneath.'

Raf pulled a towel from the drying rack and held his hand out to Tamako. 'Are we going to be first? What do you say?' The girl beamed. She was fond of her uncle Raf. The last couple of days he had become her very own BCS, her beasty-cuddle-shark. Raf had invented a whimsical pool creature. One minute it would invite cuddles and offer tours on its back, only to change its mind the next and throw its unsuspecting passengers mercilessly back into the water. Tamako could not get enough of the game.

'Have you got her arm bands, Raf, those blow up thingies?'

'They're down by the pool, auntie Em.'

'I see, good. Right, why don't you two go down and harass the swimmers? Your mum and I will be right there.'

Raf opened the gate and walked down the stairs holding Tamako by the hand.

'Right, mister.' I put Takuya on the cushion on the day bed and prepared myself for my greasing duty. He seemed to know what was expected of him as he wildly threw his leg in the air.

'Blimey, Tak, I nearly lost an eye. You rascal!' I tickled his fat tummy, it made him roar with laughter. 'Right, fella, are we going to get oiled up, or what?'

Ayane was trying to get away from the BCS. Tamako, who noticed how the fearsome beast was slowly but surely overtaking her mother, screeched in pretend terror.

'Mum! Watch out! He's behind you!'

Ayane acted all innocent. 'What was that, honey? Who did you say?'

'The shark! The BCS!'

Takuya was sitting stark naked in between my legs on the sun lounger. He looked positively mummified in his factor fifty. Mesmerised by all the commotion in the pool, he responded to his sister's shrieks with his own monotonous call, like a peacock in mating season.

'What is it? Would you like to join in, bibsee? Would you?' Ayane, having just about escaped from the beast, which had now switched all its attention onto the young girl, pulled herself up by the side of the pool. Standing up, the water came to just above her shoulders, she was leaning over the side suspended by her elbows. 'What? Are you going to seduce the big bad shark too? Yes? Do you want to be in the water with mummy, beebee, do you?' Takuya's screams had reached their highest pitch. His exuberant bounces made it difficult for me to hold on to him.

'Shall we? Takkoo-bear? What do you reckon?' But he had no time for me, his eyes were fixed on his mother.

I stood up with Takuya in my arms, he was furiously flailing.

'Yes, teddy, it's OK, your turn now,' I said, while I held him up in the air. I bent down.

'It's fine, you can let go, Em.' Ayane stretched on her tiptoes, clapped her hands.

'You coming to mummy? Yea?'

'Careful, Aya, he's as slippery as an eel. Yippie, there we go!'

The baby slithered out of my hands into his mothers. Then he slipped on further, through her hands into the water. It is what I would revisit more than anything later: did he slip through my hands or Ayane's? As if it mattered.

The baby slipped into the water and went under. One moment. A fraction of a moment. One second? Two, at the most. He immediately resurfaced. By then Ayane had him firmly in her grip again.

Takuya's shocked little face, eyes wide open, gasping for air, in Ayane's arms again, thank God, *O God, shit, that was close,* she says, and while she says it, he stretches his body again, a forceful rebound movement, a jerk, a spasm, a flinch, with all his might he fights the water, in a reflex, in primal fear, a jolt, no, not under again, his small compact body all tensed up, clenched, as he bangs the back of his head against the side of the pool, ever so briefly, ever so briefly.

A dull thump. No more than that.

'Ouch, little man.' Ayane gently rubbed her son's wet crown, he briefly looked at her, baffled and started to cry. 'Ow, ow, honey, it's ok. Did that frighten you? Shhhh, it's ok, Bibsee, we'll get out. It's ok. There, there.' I was still kneeling down by the deep side of the pool. 'Hand him to me Aya, it's fine.' But my friend had already started to wade towards the shallow end with the steps. Had she not heard me? Did she no longer trust my grip? She'd only just reached the edge of the pool and was standing firmly on dry land when all of a sudden Takuya stopped crying and threw up a big blob of greyish matter; the half-digested porridge was dribbling over Ayane's shoulder. Takuya nodded, cleared his throat and immediately started to cry again. I hurried towards my friend with a towel in hand. 'Come, put him on the chair under the parasol.' Ayane avoided my eyes as she placed her boy on the deckchair where he'd been bouncing by my side moments earlier.

With one hand she supported his little head and back, in the other she held the towel with which she wiped his mouth and face. He stopped his plaintive crying for a moment and threw up again, a smaller amount this time landed on the towel. 'Oh, my boy, what's all this, hey?' Ayane did look at me now. In her eyes I read pure panic. Raf and Tamako had come out of the pool too, hand in hand they walked towards us. 'Everything ok?' I told Raf briefly what had happened; when I got to the part where Takuya had bumped his head, Ayane screamed for her husband, as if my account of the facts had given her an idea. 'Luc, can you come out here please?' Luc would know what to do. 'Can you go get him, Raf?' I stroked Takuya's cheek. He had now vomited for the third time and his crying was becoming more laboured, he seemed to lack the energy to get up to anything like his familiar volume. Ayane looked away from me as she spoke. 'Emma?'
'Yes?'
'This isn't good, is it? Should we ring a doctor?'
'He did take a fright, that's for sure and with the throwing up, yes, I guess perhaps we should get him checked out, you know, to be on the safe side?'
Luc came running towards us, mobile phone in hand. 'What happened?' Again, I described in detail the last fifteen minutes by the pool but before I could finish Ayane interrupted me again. 'Make that phone call, come on! All this dithering, for God's sake!' As she looked away and turned to Takuya her eyes and voice softened. 'Takuya? You ok, bear? Come on, don't close your eyes, honey. Look at mummy, Bipsee!'

My normally so boisterous godson was slumped on the deck chair, he made a feeble sound that came close to humming. Luc rang 1-1-8, the national medical emergency service. He reported calmly and in fluent English what had happened. But his frustration grew fast; the person on the other end of the line was clearly more linguistically challenged.

'No, San Teodoro! Yes, Sardegna, yes, that's right. The hospital in Olbia? Is that what you say? And then what? We're miles away from Olbia? *We-are-far-away-from-Olbia*, segnora, that's what I am saying. I see, over the phone, thank you, I will.'

Luc ended the phone call and started to swear. I came and sat next to him. From the corner of my eye I saw Ayane walk up the stairs with her son in her arms, fleeing the heat on the terrace no doubt. Raf and Tamako followed her in silence.

'Shall I ring, Luc? You go upstairs.'

'No. Try Google the nearest helicopter base on your iPhone, will you? You had good connection in the garden you said?'

'Sure, but a helicopter, do you really think we need...'

'Hello, yes, is this the accident and emergency department at Olbia Hospital?' Luc held his hand over the phone. 'Do it, just in case.'

'Yes, hi, I was told to ring you, my son has had a small accident in the pool, we're on holiday in San Teodoro.' As I walked to my room to retrieve my iPhone I could hear Luc patiently answer all the questions they were putting to him. They seemed to take him seriously. But then, why wouldn't they? A small accident. For all they knew, a child was bleeding to death out there. What if he had concussion or a skull fracture? That delicate little head of his. 'About fifteen, twenty minutes. Yes, twice. No sorry, three times. He did, yes. Rather fiercely at first, then less so, more, how shall I say, quieter? Hang on. Just give me a second.' I followed Luc up the stairs. His wife was sitting on the couch with the boy on her lap.

'Is he sleepy, Aya?'

In the bedroom I found Raf and Tamako. He was sitting on one of the single beds with her, they were laying out the memory cards together. Less than three quarters of an hour ago he had been lying there, snoring. He looked a bit helpless as he turned away from the girl and spoke to me. 'She asked me to keep her occupied.' I nodded.

'Is Takuya going to hospital, auntie Em?' My hands were trembling as I unplugged the phone from its charger. 'Perhaps, *Tammeke*, to see if he's hurt himself. You play nicely with uncle Raf, all right?'

Luc drove. Ayane and I were on the back seat with Takuya in between us. She had insisted that I'd come along and sit next to the child, it was unspoken but I was to monitor Takuya alongside her. She did not say much anyhow, just made curt gestures.

Luc looked at me through the rear mirror. 'And they've been notified, yes?'

'Yes, they will be waiting for us and they were going to try to gather a medical emergency team.' We were on our way to the private helicopter base of Porto Cervo. From there on we'd be flown to the hospital in Olbia, which would take about fifteen minutes. The one in Alghero was bigger but about half an hour flight away. It did not have a helipad either, so it wasn't an option.

'Try?'

'That's what they said.' I made the information sound very matter of fact, trying not to let panic colour my voice but Ayane flinched at my every word. I knew she wanted to shut us up or silence us with some nonsensical chanting, as a child would do to block out the adult's wisdom, a finger in each ear.

'I told them we'd be there in about half an hour.'

'Definitely, traffic's fine, that's good.' He glanced once again into the mirror, this time to my right and a little lower.

Luc looked at his son who was slumped in his seat, making small weary noises; his eyes were half closed.

Forty minutes later we arrived at the helipad of 'Villa La Contra' in Porto Cervo. In front of an open helicopter two men and a woman in white coats stood gesturing and talking in Italian. A third man in jeans and shirt was standing on the bottom step of the machine looking at his watch. I assumed he was the pilot. The scene bore the weighty urgency I recognised from action film sets and I had to remind myself that this was real and that it was about us.

Again, my stomach churned and I felt like I needed to throw up. Luc was the first one out of the car. The younger of the two men ran towards him. There was no formal greeting or shaking of hands and by the look of it not even renewed interest in the chronology of events, just a measured nod while he put a firm hand on Luc's shoulder to guide him towards the helicopter. Meanwhile the other man in white, a burly middle-aged man, had made his way to the car and was opening the back door. He stuck his grey head inside. 'The baby?' Ayane just looked at him, her son seemed fast asleep. Carefully the man lifted the boy from the seat and rushed him towards the helicopter where the young woman took over, wrapping Takuya in a blanket while she walked up the steps and into the cockpit, her long, black pony tail frivolously dancing in the wind. Luc was still standing in the door opening, he ignored the woman with the bundle, instead screamed something at me or his wife, at the top of his voice but I could not make it out. Ayane kept looking from the car to the helicopter as though she was trying to recall the connection or as if she could not remember which of the two held her boy. The pilot had started the engine, the rotor blades were spinning and made a deafening noise. Ayane and I looked helplessly at the roaring vehicle. The young man in the white coat ran away from the helicopter into a nearby pavilion. The grey man was gesturing with both hands, urging us to come, his voice was stronger than Luc's as he shouted: 'You come, yes? We go!'

I was given the seat next to the pilot. Luc sat behind me with Ayane to his right. Takuya was lying on a fold out seat in between his mother and the grey man, doctor Campi. 'Arturo Campi is a plastic surgeon connected to the Ospedale Civile in Alghero', the pilot had explained. 'He has holiday home in Aldia Bianca.' We had been lucky that they'd been able to get hold of him. He happened to be on his way to Porto Cervo and had volunteered to accompany us as soon as he heard. I glanced over my shoulder. Doctor Campi was wearing headphones and spoke into his mouth piece. 'He's keeping contact with the hospital in Olbia, where we're going,' the pilot said. Immediately after take-off doctor Campi had asked the parents again to go over the details of the accident. Ayane had sounded almost apologetic. 'Nothing dramatic really, doctor, however he did swallow quite a bit of water and took a real fright when he bumped his head against the side of the pool.' Over my shoulder I saw how she looked the surgeon in the eyes as she pleaded with him. 'It was ever so slight, the bump.' The doctor did not reply but put an oxygen mask on Takuya's sleeping face and a clip on one of his little index fingers. I recalled the wonder of his miniature hand gripping mine the very first time I held him. Ayane looked at her husband, helplessly. Do something. 'Is he in danger, doctor?' Luc asked. 'Everything depends on how quickly we get him to the emergency department.' He had a thick Italian accent, there was something earthy about him I found attractive. 'He will need to be intubated. Unfortunately, this is not a medical helicopter, we cannot do that here. My apologies sir, I must speak with the hospital now.'

'Of course.' Luc squeezed his wife's hand; with the other one she was stroking her son's little fingers where the saturation clip was measuring the amount of oxygen in his blood.

I tried not to listen to what the surgeon was communicating to the hospital, luckily the sound of the motors made that easier. But I could not help catching bits of the conversation, I spoke enough Spanish to follow the broad lines of the Italian. 'Si...no... si. D'accordo. Naturalmente, si. Alora, ...dilatazione unilaterale della pupilla.' This was about Takuya's pupils, were they dilated on one side? I knew a head trauma could cause that. A bleed in the head. God, no, stop. What did I know about these things? Initial symptoms were often alarming, a lump, loss of blood or consciousness and often things would turn out all right in the end. There was so much they could do, nowadays. And so much they couldn't. A head. A child's head. 'Takuya, hello!' Was he trying to wake our boy up? 'Bradicardia.' What was that? I turned my head, did my best to avoid Dr. Campi and the fold out seat he was studying. The view to the left was possibly even more distressing. Ayane's head was lolling against Luc's chest, her face an unrecognisable grimace. She made no sound but the tears were running over her cheeks. When she saw me looking at her she buried her face deeper into her husband's T-shirt. Her hand was still resting on her son's. Was he asleep? Was he unconscious? In a coma? But surely that was unthinkable, Ayane was right, that bump hadn't seemed anything. There had to be some other explanation.

Luc stared stoically at the breath-taking scenery. We were descending. His lips were moving, was he praying? 'Aumento della pressione sanguigna....no, midriasi bilaterale per adesso, no. Si, prego. Cinque, quattro minuti.' Four, five more minutes, thank God, we were there, everything was going to be all right.

As soon as we landed and the doors of our helicopter swung open everything accelerated. Medical personnel, men and women in white came swarming towards us. My godson was lying in the middle of the helipad on an enormous stretcher. He looked pale and still, dwarfed by meters of superfluous canvas, on his brand new makeshift bed. Someone was forcing a tube into his mouth; when it looked like they were satisfied with its position someone else nodded and they rushed off with the stretcher, all the nurses and doctors conversing in clipped, austere syllables, in a language, I then understood, that spoke of life and death.

But by far the most unbearable image was that of my friend being pushed aside by a small chubby nurse with a kind, compassionate face. She firmly held on to Ayane who, still mute, was fiercely struggling to get free, wriggling with all her might, finally snapping she fell forward, like a broken twig, on her knees. She found her voice and started to yell her son's name.
I can still hear it, how she shouted *Takuya*, screamed it, at the top of her voice, while the stretcher disappeared behind those big, red swinging doors.

The three of us were sitting in a small waiting room near the emergency unit. After her outburst Luc had helped his wife to get up and we'd followed the nurse. Ayane kept trying to force her way into the treatment room into which her son's stretcher had disappeared. 'He will need me when he wakes up, he won't know where he is, please, nurse?' But none of us were allowed through the closed doors of the trauma unit.

In my trade emotions could be recycled. I had always believed it made them less random, less gratuitous. It had been one of the attractions of becoming an actor. At least *my* shit would be re-used, it would make my joys and sorrows less fleeting. But lately I had felt there was something cheap about that theory. Perhaps it was not altogether true. What if my emotional sanity was hindered by this vulture-feed? Sometimes the warmed-up pain felt more real than the original. Faced with real life suffering I'd often not felt much at all. Later, much later, the memory would wash up a suitable degree of sentiment. As if, safely lodged in its archaic form, the trauma was able to reconnect to its source.

When the door of the waiting room opened, I knew. In the hours and days to come, this knowledge would momentarily escape me.
Ayane jumped up, Luc a fraction later. The young trauma doctor avoided their eyes.
'I am so very sorry,' he said, as he ran his hand though his hair.
'That's ok, doctor,' Ayane said, 'We did not mind waiting.' Later none of us would remember what he had looked like, only that he'd been too young for this ordeal.
'We have done everything...' Ayane positioned herself right in front of him, her face nearly touching his. She took his hands in hers and started to

shake them vigorously. 'No, listen, please doctor, please, go back in there...' The doctor freed his hands and took Ayane's in a bold, brave move, this time he did look into her eyes. He spoke with a heavy Italian accent, composed and resolute, as if he were addressing a child. I remember thinking: he's good for one so young. 'Madam, it was already too late when your son arrived at the hospital. We were able to intubate immediately but immediately after we could not find a heartbeat. We tried to reanimate but...I am so, so sorry. Your little boy died of an epidural hematoma, a bleeding in the brain.' *Your little boy.* That had to be Takuya. Apparently, he was no longer alive. Maybe it was the language, maybe they meant something else. Didn't Italians often struggle with English?

'Luc?' Ayane touched Luc's arm. He had to do something.
'I don't understand', Luc mumbled in a thin voice. I got up and walked to my friend. I hesitated at first but forced myself to lift my hand and touch her; she shrugged it off.
'Don't touch me.'
'Aya?'
'Shhhh, Leave her, Emma.'
She fixed the young physician with a hard stare. 'I don't believe you. I want to see him.' The man averted his eyes. 'Where is he? What have you done with him?' She looked at her husband. 'Luc?'
'Ayane, I...' Luc looked as if he was about to faint. I guided him back to one of the chairs.
'Are you coming, Luc?' Slowly she turned towards me, her lips started to tremble. 'How about you, Emma?' Until that moment I had feared one thing more than Takuya dying: that his mother might blame me.
'Yes, ok.' It sounded neutral, as if I agreed to clear the dishes.
I was wrongly cast. I couldn't feel a thing, this was not actually happening. Any minute now someone would walk in and shout 'cut'. An extra in a white coat would take a seat in the improvised waiting area, light a fag and say: 'Better?' If not, a real doctor would appear in the doorway, out of breath. He'd let us know they had decided to carry on reanimating Taki after all and had been able to save him, that *our little boy* was doing fine but that they would need to keep him in for the night to monitor him, but that he was going to be fine, he was a child, after all, children recover whilst you're looking at them.

But he did not.

When Ayane and Luc had calmed down a little, the doctor had taken us to a small office. He wanted to tell us exactly what had happened. My intuition was that he felt he needed to give us some space, create a buffer between the shock of the message and the confrontation with our child who was no longer there.

Takuya did not *exist* anymore, or would do so, from now on, in our thoughts only. I had always found that such a hollow expression. I now realised it was the only one.

Come away, O human child!
To the waters and the wild
With a faery, hand in hand,
for the world's more full of weeping than you can understand.

WB Yeats

I had so wanted it, needed it.

A pure image. A peaceful reminder. A sign.

A glimpse of unpolluted Takuya-essence to draw comfort from, if that was how it worked. I so wanted it to seem as if he was asleep, but it didn't. Deprived of his breath, Takuya no longer looked like the boy he had been. His was the second dead body I had seen. The remains of my robust grandfather had not looked like a sleeping version of his previous self either. Even without a God to explain it all, the total person was definitely more than the sum of its parts.

Ayane was by far the bravest of the three of us. She leaned over her son's blank body. He was still lying on the stretcher which he'd been transferred to no more than forty minutes ago, dying as it turned out. Who would have thought: Takuya's final bed, a rudimentary wooden plank at Olbia-hospital's A&E department on the Italian island of Sardinia? Without Albert, his cherished little lamb, his favourite *knuffel* or the comfort of his *tutje*, the dummy without which, to his parent's dismay, he still refused to go to sleep, had refused. Present was turning into past and for now all it was, was grotesque.

She cautiously kissed his little forehead. 'Oh.' She held back, a fraction. 'You're cold, Bipsee. Feel this, Luc, how strange.' Luc stood beside her, he nodded. I saw how he fought his tears, with all his might, his lips contracted into a straight horizontal line, as did his eyes, which almost resembled his wife's. 'Strange, yes', he said in an uncharacteristically high voice, as he touched Takuya's white cheek, whereupon he sank into one of the chairs at the foot of the stretcher and started to shake, his head held in his hands. 'How can this be? This is not possible, is it? *Allez*, our *Takske*, how is this possible? Our boy with his...'

'Shh, Luc, it's ok.' I stroked his hair. 'With his...his...' But he couldn't finish the thought; each time his voice was cut off by the weight of this incomprehension.

'His what, Luc? Go on,' I said, it felt inappropriate but I so wanted to know.

'His Taekwondo-screams!' Luc cried like someone who seldom does. Like most men do: a lament of unrehearsed throaty sounds, like 'Fado', in which feelings of irreplaceable loss are looking for an escape.

Ayane on the other hand was in a trance, she hardly seemed to notice our presence. She was inspecting every inch of her dead child, a half smile on her face, talking to him and asking him questions about what he'd been through, as if, any moment now, he would respond in his own primitive way. 'Did they massage your little heart, son? Was that scary then, hey? Let mummy have a look. Oh, my baby, you've got lots of little bruises here, dear-o-dear.' She had pulled up his Toy Story T-shirt and was stroking his little chest. 'Is this where they've pushed, is it son? But you're not hurting anymore, are you? No. Thank God for that.'

How much had he been aware of? What had he experienced in those last few hours? I wondered. But the words were no longer relevant. Experience was what the living did, whose sensations were still connected to their heartbeat and this world. A world to speak about, or sing or screech about. Takuya would never tell us anything anymore. Oh God, the thought. We'd never hear him roar again or whimper or scream, nor would we ever hear him speak. He'd never call Ayane 'mummy' or point at his sister and try out Tak-versions of her tricky name. I'd never be auntie Em. For ever and a day I'd be godmother to a fourteen-month-old little boy. A doomed little boy.

I couldn't allow these cruel thoughts. I needed to be there for Ayane and Luc as they would wake up to this nightmare time and time again, after each fleeting spell of dosing respite. Thank God Raf was with Tamako. Shit, Raf! I hadn't even thought of him. He still didn't know anything. Oh God and then there was Tamako.

I kissed Takuya's cold cheek. It seemed so long ago he had stuffed it with juicy morsels of fruit, happy amongst his people, seated on the canvas in his nappy.

'Goodbye, my little bear. Take care, ok? I love you. I will always love you.' I had never meant it more. My own words caused me to weep. It wasn't sentiment, but fear. How I dreaded this new absolute circumstance; with the words came the realisation I would never again be able to address *him,* rather than this bereft Takuya-container. One last time I pressed my face into his soft little neck. His scent was gone already, he didn't smell of anything. But I knew even that would be temporary. Time to go and take my morbid thoughts with me. I pulled the door of the trauma room to leave Ayane and Luc with their son. In a little while they too would close this door and nothing would ever be what it had been.

Back in the waiting area I phoned Raf. As I heard the phone ring in the San Teodoro house, I looked up at the picture on the wall, a framed aerial view of the island. Half an hour ago I had looked at it, frightened, yet hopeful. I knew none of us would escape this reflex, the inevitable 'before-and-after-Takuya'-associations. *Exactly twenty-four hours ago we walked this path in search of Albert. The last time we went past this store, Takuya had a mighty tantrum.* Later I would learn my friend would take this habit a bit further and calculate the exact amount of living hours her boy had left at any given time.
'It's me.'
'Emma, everything ok there? How's Takuya?'
'Raf, he, it's not good. Takuya...' I held the mobile a bit away from me and blew my nose.
'Em, what's going on?' I was Em once more, it must be serious.
'Is Tamako with you?'
'Of course she is.'
'I mean, can she hear you?'
'No, she's watching *Pirates of the Caribbean*.'
'He's dead, Raf. Takuya is dead.' The words tasted strange on my tongue, these chime-less words. For a moment silence at the other end.
'What? Oh God. No! Oh, my God, Emma, he's not. But how? Oh God, no. But what then? His head?'
'Yes, his head. He suffered an epidural haematoma, a brain bleed. It can be caused by a relatively minor bump, like in Takuya's case, this afternoon.' I felt an overwhelming need to say his name. Was this a way to keep him with me?
'Jesus, Em, I can't believe this.'
'I know, me neither.'
'How are Ayane and Luc?'
'Oh, Raf, they're all over the place. I don't think it has sunk in yet, they're still in shock. They both look crushed. Just now Ayane was standing by Takuya's...' I felt the air being squeezed out of my throat.

117

'What was that?'

'Never mind, I will tell you later. Listen, don't say anything to Tamako, all right?'

'And what if she asks?'

'Just say her brother is very ill. I think this should come from her parents.'

'You're probably right. Oh shit. I can't get my head round this. Our little Takuya. When are you coming back?'

'Later tonight. The hospital has arranged transport for me and accommodation in Olbia for Aya and Luc.'

'Why is that?'

'There's going to be an inquest.'

'What?' Raf's voice went up a notch. In the background I heard Tamako jump up from her pirate story. 'Uncle Raf, is that my mummy?'

'No, honey, it's your auntie Em.'

'Is mummy coming home soon?'

'I'll be right with you, ok?'

'Can I speak to auntie Em?'

'We've got to talk a bit more but after that I'll come and sit with you. Just watch your film so you can tell me about it, all right?'

'Ok.'

'What was that about an inquest?'

'That seems to be the routine when there's been an unnatural cause of death. Understandable, if you come to think of it. Neither Ayane nor Luc is prepared to leave Takuya behind in Olbia on his own.'

'I understand. When will I see you?'

'In about an hour.'

'Em?'

'Yes?'

'Take care.'

'Thanks.'

When I got out of the taxi Raf was waiting for me. He took me in his arms, I was grateful for that.

I sighed and for a moment I found solace in his embrace. He held on to me and looked into my eyes. 'Oh, Emma, damn.' His were filling up with tears. I was cried out, for the time being. In the taxi on the way to the villa I had surrendered to my grief. The driver, who knew what had happened, had been very sympathetic. 'You ok, signora?' he asked and shook his head. 'Sad, so sad.' Without any self-censorship I had given into the torture of Takuya images, mental pictures which brought him back so vividly. It was odd, how I could control this and at the same time could not. The process was compulsive. Every new Takuya-memory brought about a new wave of heart ache. It was a form of emotional retching: waves of pain and disbelief would alternate. Like puke and cold sweat.

Takuya, the very first time I was allowed to baby sit, smiling from ear to ear when I lifted him out of his cot after he'd been screaming as if he was about to be murdered.

With Takuya and Ayane in Ostend, during a hot June weekend; baby boy in a sling, asleep on my tummy as Ayane had not yet been able to carry him like that after her Caesarean. For once she had a valid excuse to encourage my bond with my godson.

Takuya at the breakfast table on our first morning in San Teodoro, the eruption of his delirious war cry upon the discovery of dipped *speculaas*, one of his dad's greatest culinary delights.

I already knew it had a function, this masochistic probing of the heart wound, until the pus would come out. But this was different from the immeasurable sorrow I had felt after my last miscarriage and different anyhow from the stolen hope for a child of my own. Deep down I knew the difference was about more than losing a child I'd known for over fourteen months as opposed to the unnamed babies who would never have personalities, nor provide me with life-filled images to remember them by. This was something I had come to realise in the taxi.

Waves of pain and disbelief, indeed.
But also of guilt.
The difference was guilt.

I never should have handed Takuya to his mum. I should have realised he was far too slippery. It had been up to me and me only to assess that. I know. I know, he could *not* have slid through his mother's hands, *not* jolted backwards, *not* hit his head against the pool's edge. But that didn't matter. He had.

And I had been the catalyst.

I had been the very first of the falling dominos.

I had delivered the opening shot in Takuya's execution.

No one would say it out loud. Not Luc, not Raf. Even Ayane would remain noble in her heartbreak. Nonetheless, here it was, the core of my penance: living with this ultimate failing. Living with this guilt.

That night I hardly slept. I kept reliving the past twenty-four hours. Over and over, again and again. Especially from the time immediately after our siesta. From the shower up to the hospital and the parting from Takuya's pale, odourless body.

You can start greasing up that piglet of yours. You will join us, won't you? I've already got mine on underneath. You rascal! Are we going to get oiled up, or what? Would you like to join in? Careful, he's as slippery as an eel. Oh, shit, that was close. Ouch, little man. The baby? I am so very sorry. We have done everything.

If I concentrated hard enough I could invent an alternative ending. First I needed to turn back the clock. This time travel, right up to the moment of the accident, seemed to create a virtual history, an alternative past where things could be done differently. Or not done at all.

So much more was I filled with the memory of a living Takuya than the reality of his cold remains on the stretcher. It did not seem farfetched; this could be possible, as if it concerned a film script in the hands of an omnipotent director and I was the omnipotent director. My mind kept battling with the distorted reality of his death. It was so busy in my head. It felt like the hard drive of a corrupted laptop, whirring, humming, struggling to process the most basic information, all the while sending out little hour glass icons. There were moments when I was not sure of anything anymore. Then Ayane's face would appear, her arms stretched out towards me and the whole thing would crash.

Raf was dosing next to me, a suitable distance separated our bodies. He had been the one to suggest sharing the bed; it hadn't sounded like frivolous proposition.

'Come on, move over, you shouldn't be alone tonight.'

'Is that wise?'

'Listen, I haven't stopped caring about you, you know? It's not something I can just switch off like that. I want to be there when you wake up.'

'Fat chance. I won't sleep.'

'You might in the end, you're exhausted. Don't put up a fight now, kiddo, the world's bigger than you for the moment.'

He was right. How petty these worries seemed now, whether or not to share a bed or *a house and stuff*. What to do with the rest of my life?

At four in the morning I woke up from a light sleep. It felt like a punch in the stomach when the truth resurfaced: Takuya had died and was lying cold on a stretcher in Olbia.

'Raf!'

'What? What is it?'

'Takuya!' I threw his name against the walls of the half-lit room, loud and panicky. Our idyllic holiday room, where the curtains blew softly and the smell of the sea came wafting in, with its pointless view and its wretched balcony.

'Shhh, come here, it's ok, let's not wake up Tamako, honey, come here.'

Tamako. I had desperately cuddled last night and managed to avoid her inquisition, insisting I needed to sleep, that tomorrow we'd go and see mummy and daddy...and Takuya.

I nestled into Raf's warm chest. It felt safe and familiar. I sobbed quietly. Eventually, after a while the sobbing subsided and the pain eased, ever so slightly.

'He looked so vulnerable, Raf. Smaller than he was even, on that stretcher. God, that thing was far too big for our little man.' Raf's hand brushed through my hair. For a while we lay together in silence.

'Do you know that poem 'Death and the Gardener'?

'Don't think so, how does it go?'

I grabbed a tissue from the little box on the side table, blew my nose and relaxed back into Raf's body. He threw a protective arm over me. Apart from my T-shirt, things were the way they'd always been.

'It's about a Persian nobleman, whose gardener comes running into the house one day, claiming he's seen Death whilst he was pruning the roses.'

'He thinks he's dying, he thinks it's a sign, does he?'

'Hang on a minute. He senses his time has come, indeed; it also happened that Death waved at him. They're metaphors, ok, Raf? Anyhow, the gardener wants to outwit Death and so he asks his master if he can borrow a horse. He wants to run away from his fate, you see. So, his master lends him a horse and the gardener flees to Ispahan.'

'Where is that?'

'In what used to be Persia, nowadays Iran.'

'How do you know all that stuff?'

'Never mind, just listen to the story.' Raf was playing with a lock of my hair, winding it around his finger, a gesture from long ago. 'Later that day the nobleman bumps into Death. Why did you threaten my gardener this morning, he asks. Whereupon Death replies: It was no threat, sir. *But surprised I was to find in early morn, here still at work a man who, this same evening, I am to take in Ispahan.'*

'I see, yes, fate.'

'Exactly. The *moros* of the ancient Greeks, the spirit of doom that drives a man towards his fate.'

'Oedipus who consults the oracle and wants to prevent the murder of his father, flees to Thebes...'

'...and kills Laius, who turns out to be his father and marries the woman, who, unbeknown to him, is his own mother.'

'Mmm.'

'Can you imagine?' I looked at Raf.

'What?'

'Just imagine that this happened to be Takuya's fate, to live for fourteen months, to crawl, then walk for a bit. Imagine death was upon him all along, despite factor fifty, my doomed grip around his greasy body and Ayane's out-stretched arms?

'Emma, stop.'

'If not for our failing grip he would have wormed open the gate with his little, wriggly fingers and fallen down the stairs to the pool, right?'

'Emma! Enough.'

'We'd have found him in his little bed this morning, in Luc and Ayane's room, yet another sudden infant death for the statistics, a tragedy without an explanation. How will we ever know, Raf? Tell me? How will we ever know what would have happened if we'd been able to avoid this scenario?'

'You need to stop this.'

'Stop what exactly?'

'An accident has happened. That's it, Emma. A terrible, unbearable, fatal accident. Oh, God, here we go again.'

'What do you mean?'

'There is no guilt, no if-only. Why do you always do this?'

'Do what? What is this thing I do? What do you mean: *there we go again*?'

'This all this sounds so familiar.'

'You mean with regard to us?'

'It doesn't matter. Not now, anyway, not again.'

'You mean our baby girl?'

'Yes.'

'But I have not thought about that for a second, honestly, Raf, I swear to you, not for one second!'

'I believe you. But that's the difference between us you see. Don't you get it?'

'I'm not with you, Raf, honest to God.'

'Shit happens, ok? Dreadful, cruel shit. Badly timed responses, fights that run out of hand, deadly accidents, hell Em, they don't happen to contrast the boring stuff, to create a climax, life's not a theatre!'

He couldn't help it. He didn't get it. He did not understand my need to stop the ringing in my ears, to stop the guilt ringing in my ears.

Look how she survives,
Cut off and chooses direction.
Hear her diluted scream,
From far too many mouths.

Anna Enquist

I was brushing my teeth when the phone went, Raf brought it through to the bathroom. He held his hand over the mouth piece. 'It's Luc for you, I think it's about Ayane.'

My first impulse was panic. *The inquest, everything will come out. Ayane has given them the facts, that's it, I'm done.*

'Luc?'

'Hi Emma.'

'Where are you, honey?'

'At the hotel, mostly making phone calls. It looks like we're not going to make tomorrow's flight, at least not with Takuya. God. I hadn't even thought about that. Takuya's little corpse would have to be transported to Belgium. We were all meant to fly back home early evening the next day.

'Is there anything I can do, Luc? Shall I ring *Europ Assistance* or *Alitalia*?'

'No, I've done that. I've been up all night, spoken to God knows how many people, been on the Internet. I need to keep busy, Em or I'll crack up.'

'Of course, I understand. How about Aya,' I tried carefully.

'Well, that's why I'm phoning, really. I wondered if...'

'What? Tell me, anything.'

'I wondered if you could come.'

'But of course I can.'

'I can't get through to her, Emma. She seems to look straight through me.'

'What makes you think it will be any different with me?

'She calls out your name, every now and then and asks me when you're coming.' There it was. She wanted her baby back. The baby I'd taken from her. She wanted to get things straight, settle the bill.

'Did you tell her you were going to ring me?'

'Yes. It was the only thing that got her attention, it pulled her out of her lethargy for a moment. You two have a connection. A different kind of connection, I mean.'

Luc did not know what had really happened, he'd been reading in the back yard.

'Tell her I'm on my way.'

'Ayane?' The pale mask of her face lit up when she opened the door of her hotel room. She held out her arms. *God no, not that gesture.*

'Emma.' I embraced my friend, who in turn threw her arms around me, ever so lightly, as if she feared one of us might break. We normally only did firm cuddles, us feisty girls. Now my friend felt like the delicate little Japanese doll she normally only resembled in looks. Was it her mind or her battered body that had started to signal this vulnerability to her muscles?

'Oh, Aya.'

Luc sat on the bed, he was on the phone speaking English. The room smelt stale. Outside it was stiflingly hot but apparently, they had had no air-conditioning in the room or had failed to switch it on.

'How is Tamako?'

'Don't you worry about her honey, uncle Raf is pampering that girl.'

'I'm sure, that's not what I mean, though. How did she take it?'

'We've not told her yet, Ayane. Only that her brother is extremely ill.'

'I see.'

'Aya?'

'What?'

'I'm not sure how to say this but: I'm so very sorry.' When I had left the hospital the day before I'd said goodbye with something similar. What could one say, after all? They were such inadequate phrases. Perhaps they were appropriate if you spilled wine on someone's favourite blouse. Or when you happened to be out of coffee. What were words doing here? But what else was there? Was it an option to remain silent in the face of the unspeakable? 'I know.' How had she interpreted mine? How about me myself? Had I referred to Takuya's dying or my part in it? Would her reply give me the answer? Ayane changed the subject.

'We were about to leave for the hospital. He's on another ward now. Are you coming?' Oh my God. 'Of course. Have you eaten anything, Aya?'

Luc was wrapping up his phone call. 'Thanks. We will.'

'Hi Emma. No, she has not and that's what we'll do first. There's a snack bar around the corner, opposite the hospital. Coffee and sandwiches, now.'

Ayane shuffled to the bathroom, her face vacant, she tuned on a tap. I gave Luc a kiss and a pat on his back. 'Ça va, *mateke*?' Luc shrugged his shoulders. He looked awful. The cold sore on his lip had now fully broken out; a heavily infected crust was blotting his upper lip. He was still in the sand coloured cotton shirt he had been wearing during yesterday's siesta in the back yard. Yesterday's siesta was light years away. Under his arm pits big discoloured rings of dried up sweat had stained the fabric. I had a change of clothes with me for both of them.

'Anyway, at least they're going to try and finalise the autopsy report by the end of the afternoon, then a legal person will come and look into it, take down our witness statements and file everything officially. So, in principle, if all goes smoothly things will be sorted out today, at least that's how I understood it.' Luc sounded manic. I'd be exactly like that. Gain control over something. I was more worried about Ayane. The invitation to come to hospital with them had sounded as if we'd be off to visit Takuya after he'd had his tonsils out. The other ward just happened to be the mortuary where he'd be lying on ice in a drawer with a number tag on his little big toe.

I felt no need to see that.

'What won't be possible, however, is take human remains on a commercial flight. Takuya will need to be repatriated at a later stage, I'm afraid.

'How soon can they do that?'

'At Europ Assistance they reckon anything from five to ten days. So I guess Aya and I will have to decide whether to say here or fly out with you guys tomorrow. Not sure how to broach that subject yet.'

'Listen Luc, I'm here too, right? You want me to talk to her?'

'You're a good friend, Emma.'

I wanted to explain to him that I had to make up for something. I wanted to go over the accident with a fine-tooth comb. I needed him to be my judge. It was the last thing he needed right now. Luc filled a glass of water at the tap and drank it in one go.

'And then there's the costs. If we decide to stay here it's going to be very costly. Not that I'm losing sleep over it but the helicopter alone will cost a few thousand euros.'

'Won't that be covered by the insurance?'

'No.'

'Oh, before I forget, could you remind me to phone the Belgian Embassy in Rome later on, Emma? Unless of course the hospital already did that, which I doubt.'

His last sentence was a mere mumble. His brain was flashing back and forth, from problem to solution and back.

'Are you obliged to?'

'Yes, should have done it already, really.'

'God, Luc, I think you're incredibly brave.'

'What else can I do? Run up and down to the hospital like Ayane does?'

'She does?' He nodded sombrely. 'I can't blame her, she's climbing the walls.'

'I do understand that. She needs to tell herself he's still out there somewhere. Somehow, somewhere.'

'I know. Yesterday she came back from the hospital and they're all great there by the way, I can't fault them, anyhow, she started to complain about her breasts, that they were sore, tender. I replied with my big mouth that perhaps she had a period coming on, insensitive fool I am. How do you explain that, though? Do you think that's possible, Emma that a woman's breast start aching after the loss of a child?'

'I've heard of that before, yes. Oh God, poor Ayane.

'Luc?' The bathroom door was ajar, I shot a quick glance at my friend. She was bending over the toilet, as if she was trying to remember how to flush it. 'Yes?'

'I don't want to join you two in the mortuary, if you're ok with that.'

'Of course. Not a problem, I understand.'

'How about Ayane, won't she find that difficult?'

'Well, then she'll have to, won't she? I fear Ayane will find most things difficult now and for a long time to come.'

Ayane was standing by the sink. She stared at her tooth brush.

She began to brush her teeth, dry, without paste or water. She looked into the mirror, through the mirror and caught my face. I was standing in the doorway. She offered me a weak smile. I came in and handed her the plastic bag with the change of clothes.

'Here.'

'Thank you.'

She splashed a handful of cold water on her face and padded it dry with a towel. She began to undress. For a moment my athletic friend, whose body was usually so alert, switched on and beaming with feline grace, reminded me of my grandmother during the latter months in the care home. Stripped of self-awareness her naked body looked dull and colourless.

'Do I need to put on something else?' she asked.

'I'd say so yes, honey, these things are dirty.' I picked up the plastic bag and handed her the clean clothes. I helped her to get dressed, as if she were Tamako.

'Better, no?'

'Should we bring clean clothes for Takuya too?' The shock of her question made me nauseous. I frantically started to hang up the wet towels and cleared away the dirty laundry. There was no need to, but I flushed the toilet once more and ignored her question. I did not dare remind her. If she had temporarily blocked out what had happened it was not up to me to interfere with the way he would be laid to rest.

The house was locked in an eerie silence. How different it felt from the soporific calm we'd enjoyed during our daily siestas over the past week, which had allowed us to recharge our batteries. Tamako would do a puzzle or a drawing. Luc was usually engrossed in his laptop. Raf, who enjoyed cooking, would make initial preparations for dinner, marinade the fish or make pizzas for the kids. Ayane and I would be quietly chatting, doing each other's toe nails or reading our books. The baby would be asleep.

This was an ominous silence. The calm before the storm of renewed agony. This peace was the result of a war of attrition, of the exhausting battle with the reignited awareness of our loss.

Everything was packed. In two hours' time the cleaning team would be here and we'd hand over the keys. We'd drive to the airport in Olbia and make one last stop at the hospital, where Tamako and her mother would say their last goodbyes to Takuya. Neither Luc, Raf or I felt that we wanted to do this.

At the hospital Ayane and Luc had been tentatively advised to join the rest of us on the flight back home today. The legal person hadn't shown up yet. The police had been informed as had the Belgian Embassy. None of these instances however, had been able to shed light on the process for the release of Takuya's body and subsequent repatriation. The wait was for the autopsy report. The social worker connected to the hospital had offered my friends a type of counselling meant for those who suffered a sudden bereavement. It even had a name, SDBC was invented for people like them, like us, what a relief. The guy had advised Luc and Ayane not to travel alone and pointed out that, especially in the initial phase, the presence of both parents was crucial for the surviving child or children. Again, Ayane had wanted me there during the session. I started to feel she found it hard to be alone with her husband. In the taxi back to the house she had been crying quietly, very discretely in true Japanese style. I was relieved that she could at least do that. Luc had taken her hand in his, which she'd allowed and for a while he'd held his wife's unresponsive hand. Ayane was locked up and strangely enough I was the only one she'd allow a little closer from time to time. I was the only one she'd properly look at. With her daughter the communication would prove even less obvious. It would be Luc who'd set himself the impossible task of telling his daughter about the death of her brother.

Upon our arrival Tamako ran straight into her daddy's arms. Her mother, who'd become slower overnight, was still in the taxi. Luc held his daughter in a tight grip, took her by the hand and walked to the house. Raf had been standing by the sliding doors to the terrace. He gave Luc a firm hug and guided him inside, his hand in a fatherly gesture on his friend's shoulder. Luc immediately lead his daughter to the settee and pulled her close by his side on the seat next to him. When Ayane walked in, he beckoned her to join them. Ayane flopped down on the couch, she looked exhausted. She gave her daughter a kiss on the head and swung her arm over the girl's little shoulders. 'Hey, muppet, I hear you've been such a good girl?' The voice didn't sound like hers. Tamako looked at her mum suspiciously.
'We've missed you, *huppelke*,' Luc said. He pulled the girl closer. She was his only child now. He and Ayane suddenly had a child, not children. How weird was that? Ayane rubbed her daughter's bronzed little leg.
'Daddy, where's Takuya?' Ayane shut her eyes, tears ran down her face, where did they keep coming from? Suddenly that seemed quiet an interesting field of research: the correlation between the secretion of tears and inner turmoil. In contrast to Ayane's free-flow, the production of sound remained minimal. Did she imagine the girl hadn't picked up anything yet?
'*Tammeke*, we have to tell you something, honey', Raf said. 'Something terrible.'
'Where's my brother, mummy? Is our Takuya still in hospital?' I was still standing by the terrace doors, like a voyeur, incapable of turning my tear-stained face away from this most intimate upsetting family scene. *Our* Takuya. I suspected that must have hit my friend more than anything. The girl was right, we'd so shared him. His pure energy, his clingy little body. Tamako looked into her mother's distorted face. Suddenly Ayane could no longer remain silent and burst into a loud whine, for a moment it sounded as if Takuya had come back. She got up and hurried out onto the terrace. I followed her.

'Ayane?'

'No, I...I can't...lea... me.' She had opened the gate and was running down the stairs towards the pool. For a second there was a déjà vue of an earlier scene, that of Ayane's naked water dance. Once more she headed for the pool, weeping like a lost little girl. My heart sank. I followed her down the stairs. From the house came the sound of hysterical wailing. Tamako.

Ayane was sitting by the side of the pool, her legs dangling in the water. It was the exact same spot where we had faced each other in trepidation, two long days ago.

I kicked off my sandals and came to sit next to her, my feet in the water. Ayane's head was suspended forwards, hanging. She'd finally stopped crying and was staring into the azure water.

I gently stroked her back. 'It's ok, my love, it's ok.'

'It's not, Emma, it's not. I don't know what I'm doing. And now Tamako, I'm failing again.'

'You're not. Do you hear me?' My friend swung her legs out of the water. She clasped her arms around her knees and searched my eyes: an unspoken appeal. *Look at me.* I pulled my legs out of the water and mirrored her pose.

'What?' I asked her. She shook her head. My heart was pounding against my ribs. 'What is it?'

'What have I done?'

'You've not done anything, Aya.'

'My son is dead, Emma. I let him slip through my fingers like a bar of soap, don't tell me I didn't do anything, or do, because I did nothing, nothing whatsoever to help him!'

Oh God. *She* felt guilty. I looked at her wrung out little face, her swollen, red eyes until I could no longer take her pleading stare. I closed my eyes. I was silent for a while. When I began to speak it felt wrong again, as if I was going to give her ideas.

'If anyone should feel guilty it's me.' Did I ask her to forgive me? Was she not burdened enough?

'You?'

'I applied his sunscreen. Liberally.'

'But of course. Otherwise he would have burned.'

I too looked into the water, as if the answer was out there somewhere, along with a trace of the accident, an indication, a different perspective. I took Ayane's hand in mine. She looked up at me like a wounded animal.

I wracked my brain for Raf's mantra about coincidence and the absence of fate, of guilt. Perhaps he was right and I was looking for a coward's way out with all this mental torture. Wasn't it a form of conceit, this illusion of ultimate power over things?

'Aya, my dear friend, listen to me: it was an accident, an awful accident and it should not have happened, but it did. You were, are a wonderful, caring mother, not God. And I was a devoted godmother, Ayane, honestly, I loved him so, so much I...' I couldn't go on, I could not seem to regulate my breathing. I had clearly raked things up for her again because she too was too upset to speak. But she squeezed my hands and spoke unsteadily, through her tears.

'I knew you felt it was your fault and if I'm honest that suited me, isn't that cruel?'

'Tell me, what would you do differently, if you knew how it was going to go?'

'Nothing.'

'Exactly.'

'But I do know how it went and I'd do everything differently.'

'So would I. So would I.' She let go of my hands and put her head on her knees.

'I am so tired. So empty, so scared. I'm scared of every new hour. I can't tell Luc, I don't want to either. He's got nothing to give for the moment, there's nothing I want from him. Only for him to give me my boy back. But that he can't do.'

'I'm here, Aya, with you and I don't think for a minute I can feel what you feel, but I'm here and I want to...'

'Of course you can', she interrupted me. 'More than anyone.'

'I guess I have an idea, yes. But to feel what you feel...'

'Fuck Em, I'm not talking about degrees of intensity or weighing up losses, am I? I'm talking about the pain, the agony of a future collapsed. About having something inside you ripped out, you know, literally, snatched out of your body, an essential part of your body. You know about that. You've been blathering on about it for...' She could not talk for the tears. 'And I don't know how,' she gasped, 'or why that helps me but it bloody well does, you know, it helps that you know.'

I just nodded and kept smoothing her smooth hair, which needed a wash.

'Oh Ayane, my love.'

At the top of the stairs the gate was being unlocked. When I looked up, Luc and Tamako were already at the bottom of the steps. He looked at the girl, concerned. With trembling bottom lip Tamako ran to her mother, Ayane offered her arms, the girl fell into them, crying.

'It's ok, angel, mummy's here, it's ok.' Her voiced sounded more Ayane.

Tamako was seated in between her mother and me on the plane. Ayane had finally nodded off asleep. I rescued the plastic wine cup from her loosened grip and pushed the little pillow a bit further under her head, which was leaning against the window.

'Auntie Em?'

'Yes, my sweet?'

'Are you my godmother now?' Her question took me aback. But that was nothing new. Ever since her daddy had told her the news, she had been overflowing with questions. What did being dead feel like? What was it like to sleep in a box underneath the grass? Questions too about the blood in Takuya's head.

'But you already have a godmother, don't you, hon? Your *omoe* Hoshi?'

'Yes, I know, but what if I had a second one, wouldn't I be super protected if anything happened to mummy or daddy?'

'Mmm. Not sure. Maybe we need to discuss that together, you know, mummy, daddy and omoe Hoshi? And you and I of course. What do you reckon?'

'Ok. Do you want to play OXO with me?'

'Sure.'

Even though she seemed to respond well to the small snippets of truth and comfort we alternatingly fed her, the girl woke every morning to a word she had to reinterpret. On the way to the airport she had told me she'd accidentally ran into her parent's bedroom that morning and to her brother's bed, to wake him, excited as she had been about the flight home.

Raf was sitting on the other side of the isle. He looked at me and winked. I was frightened of what awaited me. Frightened of the divorce, of a life without him; a life without Takuya, with my best friend desperate, broken. I'd received a text message from France last night. Joris was looking forward to a night out, to sharing our respective holiday disaster-tales and washing them down with a few Duvels. I had deleted it straight away; flirty texting belonged to a previous life.

Luc and Raf were scanning the baggage carousel; every now and then they pulled off one of our cases. Tamako was sitting cross-legged at my feet, she was patiently brushing her dolly's hair. The girl had been incredibly brave, the past twenty-four hours. Perhaps the social worker was right. Despite their emotional unavailability, Luc and Ayane's presence was the only thing that mattered to her. She seemed to need regular mum or dad feel-fixes and would beg for a kiss or a cuddle or simply rub her little body against one of theirs. Both seemed to understand this and responded very protectively and tenderly.

'You ok?' Ayane looked as white as a sheet.

'Emma?'

'What is it? Are you not feeling well?' I put my hand under her arm for support, she seemed unsteady on her feet. She leaned heavily into me, then pulled herself together and took a step back.

'I want to go back. I want to fly back to Olbia.'

'Oh, my love, of course you do.' I pulled her towards me but she gave me a mean push. 'Don't bloody patronise me. I mean it. What the hell am I doing here? I left my child on an island, all on his own, this feels completely wrong!'

A few fellow travellers turned their heads.

'It's ok, honey, shhh, calm down.'

'I am calm!'

Tamako's doll was lying in her lap, the girl looked frightened, she glared up at her mum from under her fringe. A small group of passengers from the Olbia flight looked in our direction, more openly curious this time. We'd been suspended in the air together for several hours, they felt they had the right.

What was wrong with that woman? Did those two have a quarrel? En plein publique at Zaventem airport? How vulgar.

'What is it, honey?' Luc was pulling two heavy, bright yellow cases. He put them to one side and walked up to his wife, he put his hand under her elbow. 'Leave...me alone!' she shouted. The first word had sounded loud and harsh, the following two not so, almost more to herself, as if she'd suddenly realised she was in a public space.

'We are going to order a cab, is that ok Ayane?' He was articulating every syllable, as if he was addressing his daughter. My friend looked at me for advice. 'But I don't want to go home,' she sulked. 'I want to go back.'

'Ayane, sweatheart, that's not an option,' I said calmly but firmly. 'Would you rather come to my house? Together with *Tammeke*?' Ayane, looked at Luc.

'It's ok, you know, hon? If you'd rather? Would you?' He tried to encourage a solution. Ayane stared at a vague point in the distance for a while, then began to nod; she did not seem convinced but recognised defeat.

Ayane was in the bath.

Raf had accompanied Luc home. Tamako was helping me in the kitchen. The two of us had been food shopping and now, there she was, in her gigantic checked apron, on a little step by the work surface, slicing tomatoes. I'd put on her 'Cowboy Billy Boom'-cd. Quietly she sang along. *Tumba, tumba, tumba, tumba, tumba, tumba, tum-ba.* She understood all too well why her mummy had preferred to come to this house. 'Takuya is still in ours, auntie Em, even though he's dead', she cleverly pointed out.

Ayane walked into the kitchen, she was swallowed up in Raf's shaggy bath rope.

'Was that nice?' She nodded, walked behind me and planted a kiss on the nape of my neck. 'Thank you, Emma.' Her damp hair smelled of coconut.

'Come here, my brave sunflower.' Tamako put down the knife and wiped her hands on her apron, like a true little chef. She jumped from her step and pulled herself onto her mother's lap, burying her head in the soft fabric of the dressing gown. Ayane stroked her daughter's little body and kissed the girl's head. 'Mummy is very proud of you. Do you know that?' Tamako nodded, her head into her mum's bosom.

'Are we staying here for always, mummy?'

'No, hamster, we're only gathering some strength. Tomorrow we'll go home, to daddy.' She swallowed. The sentence did not feel finished.

On the day of Takuya's funeral, the rain came down in buckets. I woke up in the middle of our king- size bed having temporarily forgotten. It came back to me in a wave of fear. The force of it sucked away my breath. I could hear my own heart, hammering away in my chest. Today we would burn the little white chestnut coffin in which he was laid out, like a little pharaoh, with Albert, his favourite toy-lamb, by his side. The protocol surrounding Takuya's repatriation had stipulated that the body had to be embalmed.

I had dreamt of a child I did not know. I was carrying him around on my back, wrapped in a colourful batik, like an African woman. As I walked along a long lane, with tall willows on either side, I enjoyed the feeling of the baby's weight, of his warm body pressing into mine. After a while I started to notice how the people passing would stare at me, some pointing fingers at me. I arrived at a well and carefully bent over to drink. My reflection in the water told me that my baby was no longer there. Hurriedly I undid the batik; my baby was gone. In the middle of the batik was a big, damp patch. My baby had melted.

Through the bedroom's skylight I looked at the bleak clouds. I once read that for some African people a rainy burial was a gift from the gods. Ancestral tears would blend with those of the mourning relatives. The body's fusion with humid earth would create the optimum breeding ground for new life. Being Belgian, it meant little to me. For a moment I toyed with the idea of phoning Ayane to tell her about it, but I did not dare for fear it might be inappropriate. What I possibly dreaded more was the confrontation with the intensity of her pain.

Since our return from Sardinia Raf had slept in the spare bedroom. He was kind, on the verge of clingy. After the funeral he would go and stay with a good friend of his until he'd found a place of his own. I didn't feel too upset about it all. I seemed to lack the head space to digest our separation but I knew it was likely that the process was on hold. Raf gave the impression of wanting to leave sooner rather than later; out of fear that he might change his mind? My apparent indifference made that slightly easier.

Raf walked down the stairs in his crisp black suit.

'Morning.'

'Morning. You ok?'

'So so. Haven't slept much. What do you think, Raf?' I posed in front of him, fanning out the skirt of my green summer dress.

'I actually wanted to wear the black silk one, but somehow that felt less appropriate. You know, the one with the tassels? Do you not think this one too cheerful? Or can I get away with it?'

'Sure you can. Takuya was a little boy and a bubbly chap. No need to make a sombre occasion even darker, is there? This mossy green is not too serious but not really frivolous either, spot on.'

'Thanks.' I was relieved he did not give me any sermons about *the need to celebrate Takuya's life, instead of marking his passing away* or *feeling blessed to have known him*. I hoped no one would feel the need to go down that route today. It wasn't the sort of thing Ayane and Luc would be waiting to hear. Or was it? I had started on a poem that I intended to read out today, after the scattering of Takuya's ashes. I needed to finish it, but this was precisely my dilemma. What to emphasise more: the happy memories or the pain of his loss? Was there a way to read meaning into this tragedy?

'How exactly will this work today, you any idea?' I did not really feel like talking. Raf, on the other hand, seemed to need the illusion of 'normal'.

'You mean the sequence of the various ceremonies?'

'*Various* ceremonies?' I'd preferred not to think about it yet, to be left in peace with my own thoughts.

'I'm not sure, Raf,' I said. 'There will be a service in the crematorium. And then there is the coffee table, I presume.'

'The *coffee table*?'

'Please, Raf, don't tell me you don't know what that means?'

'Emma, I have never in my life been to a funeral. I know what a coffee table is, but what does it mean?'

'The phrase is a bit of a give-away, is it not? After the service people come together, you know, around a table of some sort, and have coffee. Or something stronger. Or they have a sandwich. Anyhow, that's how it's known in Flanders.'

'I see. And then what?'

'I guess that gives the crematorium the time to do the necessary, you know, and fill up the urn.'

'Ok.' *Ok?* Each word was sticking to my throat. I heard myself articulate robotic replies to Raf's tedious questions but still it did not fully register we were talking about my godson. His name had cropped up so often, lately. Part of me could easily un-know the reason why.

'And it's after that we go to the gardens of remembrance at the cemetery, right?'

'Yes.' That would have to do. 'What time have you booked the cab for? I need to check something.'

'About an hour. More coffee?'

'No, thanks. Umbrellas, let's not forget.'

'Em, you sure of this?' Raf glanced at his holdall. 'I'm happy to stay on, you know, after the service? A few days or so, what do you think?'

'No, it'll be fine. I'll be fine. Let's do it, bury it all at once.' I added a silly nervous laugh, it was rather tasteless.

'Emma, our bond never dies, it transforms. We'll always remain friends, right?'

The Raf I'd not be able to send away would respond with a sardonic joke, dissolving bitter with bitter, neutralising my self-indulgent remark. It was exactly what our dance was missing: light-footedness.

I took a pen and the half-finished poem out of my handbag and went to sit down at the kitchen table.

Tamako was wearing a cream-coloured summer dress I hadn't seen before. In her right hand she was holding a basket of white lilies, in her left a small white umbrella. Ayane too was from head to toe in white, apart from the purple crochet scarf around her shoulders. She looked incredibly brittle. She wore a big pair of sunglasses, to shield herself from prying looks, to allow the inevitable flow of tears today?

Luc, in jeans and black shirt, looked worn out, even more so than the last time I had seen him at the airport, almost two weeks ago. The soft head of Tamako's big teddy bear was sticking out of the plastic carrier in his hand. He greeted Raf, who was picking up Tamako to give her a hug.

'Hey my darling, you look nice.' I kissed my friend. She smiled and gave me a hug and nodded towards the road.

'Mum's arriving too.' A taxi pulled up next to our car. An elderly oriental lady got out. I hardly recognised her. I had only met Hoshi once, at Takuya's 'welcome-to-the-world celebration', an atheist variation to the traditional catholic baptism.

Hoshi was a warm hearted, short, chubby woman in her early sixties. Today she looked at least ten years older. We had rung her a few times from Sardinia, before the accident. She had sounded so proud when Takuya had finally shouted 'Hosh' through the phone. Ayane's dad had suddenly died when she was five. Her mum had never made a secret of her desire for male descendants. She herself had always longed for a son. She loved Tamako dearly, but the arrival of her first grandson had been a dream come true.

'Hi, Hoshi.' I hugged her. As ever she smelled of *Chanel Cristalle*. At my touch she began to weep, little modest shudders of grief. I felt a little uneasy, patting her frail little shoulders as if she were a little girl. 'It's all right, it's all right.' She looked at me, her face a tormented Japanese No-mask.

'You are a very good friend to our Ayane, Emma. I thank you, with all my heart.'

'And your Ayane is like a sister to me. So, you see, Hoshi, you're a little bit my mum too.'

'Yes, you're quite right my girl. My daughter.' She gave me her broadest smile, while she rearranged a strand of my hair, putting it back behind my ear. I thought of our last phone conversation from the hospital in Olbia. Ayane had held the phone more than a meter away, as her mother's heated howl came rolling into the waiting room like erupting lava, in the end I had taken the phone from her.

Hoshi was also wearing white. I was relieved to have left my black dress at home and even the green one suddenly seemed a bit gloomy. Perhaps I should have rung after all. I started to feel nervous. My mouth was bone-dry and my tummy ached. People were arriving from everywhere, in cars, on bikes, on foot. I recognised Ayane's neighbours, her GP and several women from antenatal yoga, as well as Ayane's older twin sisters. There were a number of well-known dancers, the artistic director of the Royal Ballet of Flanders, colleagues of Luc's and quite a few mums from Tamako's nursery. There were an awful lot of people I didn't know too. The car park was humming with subdued greetings. Stolen glances at the women in white.

Luc was talking to his parents Armand and Martine. I joined them and shook their hands.

'My sincere condolences, Armand, Martine.' The elderly couple nodded stiffly. They were both wearing formal, black funeral outfits. Luc's dad was a conservative man, a fanatical Flemish nationalist who worked as a tax inspector. Martine was a dedicated housewife at the service of her man. Both were dedicated grandparents, devoted to their grandchildren. Now there was one grandchild. Luc's sister, who lived in Canada and who would not be over for the service, had no children of her own, so that didn't count.

Suddenly all went quiet. A snow-white BMW entered the drive. In the back, on a little platform covered in white lilies, sat a small white coffin. On a black plaque on the lid his name was written in golden ornamental letters: Takuya. Underneath it was repeated in Japanese characters. I started to cry. I looked around me and saw I was not the only one.

I recognised the driver of the BMW as Luc's tennis partner. He opened the back of the car and carefully lifted out the little white coffin and put in the arms of his friend. Luc carried it in front of him at a rather low angle, a bit like one would bring in a drowned body from the sea, ceremonious, solemn, in awe of the life it had contained only moments earlier.

Ayane gathered a few lilies from the platform and held out her other hand to Tamako; she was now only carrying the basket. The girl looked up at her uncle Raf, who was holding the little white umbrella; he gave her an encouraging nod.

It was this slow-motion film that signalled the beginning of the actual ceremony. Gradually the crowd in the car park started to move, following the young family into the hall of the crematorium.

At the front of the hall hung a large canvas with a picture I recognised immediately, for I had taken it myself. A smiling boy in a high chair on a sun soaked terrace. The boy has big chocolate rings around his mouth, he's clapping his little hands in pure delight. In front of the canvas was a pedestal, covered in white silk, on it Luc had put his son's coffin; Ayane had draped the lilies on and around it.

It was eerily quiet in the hall.

Someone tapped against the microphone. It was Armand. He took a scrap paper from his coat pocket, unfolded it and put it in front of him on the reading stand. As soon as he started to read, it became clear he knew the short verse by heart.
'Toon Hermans,' he said, quoting the name of the writer, who was a well-known Dutch stand-up comedian turned poet. For a moment it looked as though he was going to make a slight bow, the way we used to in school upon declaring a poem in front of the class: name of the writer, title, bow and then reel off the verse. But instead Armand looked straight into the crowd and delivered his two lines in a powerful, unsentimental voice.

'Further away from the world, every day a little more.
Closer to the light, with every step a little closer to heaven's door.'

Next Armand turned his head towards the canvas, then looked at the little white coffin and said: 'So long, Takuya, see you soon.' Head down he walked up to where he and his wife were sitting. *My missis*, he called her. Luc and I had sometimes played a parody version of his mum and dad, in broad Antwerp dialect. I wasn't one for corny Hermans-poems, but I was moved by the sincerity and simplicity of Armand's last conversation with his grandson.
In the back of my mind I could hear Luc and me, in better days, joke about this: *'That'll do, won't it?'*
For Armand less was definitely more.

During the intermezzo that followed, a Lullaby Rendition of The Cure's 'Rockabye Baby', child friendly xylophone versions of the songs with which Luc had hoped to make Takuya into the kind of fervent Cure fan he was, Haru, one of Ayane's twin sisters walked to the microphone.

Apart from the short hair and the hippy clothes, she could easily have passed for my friend's younger sister. Fumiko and Haru were non-identical twins, five years Ayane's senior. With Haru, whom I only knew from pictures, Ayane had little contact. She lived in Brittany with a female friend, and taught music at the conservatoire. Ayane thought Haru might be gay, apparently not a topic that could openly be discussed in family circles.

Fumiko lived on her own in Rotterdam, in a flash ground floor apartment with lots of cats. She had an important job with a publishing company and had her own column with a prestigious literary magazine. She and Ayane met up regularly, despite the distance and they followed each other's work with interest. I had met her a few times and had found her slightly arrogant.

The three arty sisters were very different, even if Haru looked more like Ayane than her twin, who was more like her mum in shape and size.

'I will sing a medieval Breton ballad about the death of a young girl. In the song the girl receives the breath of the wind and the voice of the sea. I will sing the verses in Breton and the refrain in Japanese, for my sister Ayane and her husband Luc and for their daughter Tamako and for Takuya, of course. Without hesitation Haru began her a cappella song. Her powerful voice, which was in strong contrast with her slight frame, echoed through the hall, pure and riveting. She took generous breathing pauses, after which her voice would shoot up again, with the ease of a well-tuned instrument. The Celtic verses sounded melancholic and warm, the Japanese refrain more esoteric, but equally soulful. I saw Ayane fumble a handkerchief out of her sleeve and pat her tears, before slipping her hand back into Luc's. Tamako, who was sitting on her other side and next to me, leaned towards me and spoke whispered in my ear: 'That lady is my auntie too.'

Haru's final spellbinding notes were still in the making when her twin sister was already making her way to the microphone. It felt slightly tactless. Fumiko was, despite her short, stocky build, an attractive woman. She wore her dark, straight hair in a sophisticated, half-long cut, the kind one would find in hairdresser's magazines. She dressed in style. Haru's twin was not wearing white either, but in contrast to her sister's colourful, Indian medley, Fumiko wore a simple, lavender coloured, linen dress, with a wide, red leather belt and a short, tight, purple jacket. The outfit was matched with expensive looking, high-heeled sandals. Upon her arrival, she had embraced Ayane; the thought had occurred to me that the two sisters had made an effort to match their colour schemes. I now felt it was more likely their tastes were similar.

Fumiko skilfully lowered the microphone stand and began her eulogy. It became immediately clear this woman was used to public speaking. Like any accomplished performer she knew the secret of successful communication with an audience: speak, watch, pick up the crowd's signals and take them on board. Build up the tension and release it.

'Uninvited associations do not follow a moral code. Seldom do they offer comfort. Memories drifting in, their accompanying images forcing themselves onto our retina can be cruel and without mercy. The very first memory that assaulted me after the doomed phone call from Sardinia was this: a little black and white ultrasound photograph, held up triumphantly by my younger sister on December fifteenth, twenty months ago. Have no illusions, I looked it up. The date was ring-fenced in my diary, in thick black felt tip pen. That's to say, not Aya's fifteen-week-ultrasound-scan, but the day before. The Christmas parties at our office are legendary.

'Well. What do you see?' she asked me.

'A baby,' I think I said. I'm a lot less articulate with a hangover.

'Look, you dozy mare!' she shouted, irritated with my inadequate observations.

'I *am* looking', I said.

'Here!' She was shouting hysterically now, scraping her nail over a pinprick somewhere at the base of the tiny baby-body-to-be.

'Do you see it *now*?'

Only someone with the paranormal imagination of my sister could read into this miniscule dot the promise of what, for generations past, the entire Watanabe line had been hoping for: a willy.'

Fumiko's audience was eating from her hand. Muffled laughter whispered through the auditorium, a welcome antidote to tears. For the first time in days I saw Ayane and Luc laugh, hesitantly but disarmingly, hungry for a context in which this, however briefly, was allowed.

'I looked away from the picture, hoping for the support of a more mature adult, who, devoid of wishful thinking, would be able to call my sister to order and tell her that your average penis looks a tad more convincing than a dot the size of a grain of sand, but to my dismay I caught the dreamy expression of my brother in law. In a blink of an eye everything became clear: Luc was part of this conspiracy. If I wanted to come out of this unscathed I'd better act the fool.

'Wow!' I faked. 'A boy.'

'Pfff. Finally.' Both Ayane and Luc breathed a sigh a sigh of relief.'

'It was the deep conviction of my sister and her husband that the arrival of a son would complete their lives. Their wish, the ultimate king's wish, to be blessed with both a daughter and a son was about to come true. On the twenty-ninth of May of last year Takuya was born; he brought us all together soon after to celebrate his welcome to the world. I have never seen my younger sis more glowing. Never was she more beautiful and at one with herself then on that day. Her picture was perfect.'

'A while ago I asked Ayane about the things she still wanted to achieve in her professional life as a dancer; she had just been selected to be part of the leading dance programme *'Coupe Maison'*. She did not have to think long. 'Shit, this is going to sound very trite, Fumi', she said. 'Go on', I replied. 'Dance my children. Do you understand that? Dance what they have done to me, do to me. There's this other way in which I move since I have become a mother. Does that sound tacky?' 'It does a bit,' I said.

It's only now, Ayane, now I see you I limping along as an amputee, deprived of half of that transforming life-force you tried to describe to me, that I understand what you meant on that day.

From uncertain laughter Ayane had switched back to tears, and many with her. I too was crying, even though I had wanted to avoid that as much as I could in Tamako's presence.

'I will now read a poem by Herman de Coninck. For me he describes the core of what it means to be a parent, as far as I can judge that. The poem also touches upon the comfort of words. Words can't bring Takuya back, but they may help us to hold on to and revisit the essence of who he was. I hereby promise you Ayane, Luc, mum, Haru, Tamako, Armand and Martine and all who are here today, touched by his death: I will continue to talk about him. About his boundless energy, about his alien roaring, his Flemish-Japanese tempestuousness and his unrivalled hunger for hugs. For what has been part of so many, will always inspire.

SLEEP NOW

'Go to sleep now,' I say

to a daughter who is already asleep

and wakes from my words.

The thunder crashes. Perhaps

I want her scared, so I can be dad.

But there's nothing I can do except

do nothing, together with her.

It's like words. Things happen.

Without words they would still happen.

But then without words.

It had become increasingly quiet in the auditorium during Fumiko's speech. At the back of the hall the distant sound of musical instruments being tuned could be heard. All at once an unexpectedly lively melody emerged and to the frivolous beat of a children's song two violinists and a clarinet player made their way to the front through the centre aisle. Along the way the happy tune altered into something altogether more feverish, almost gypsy-like, a bit like a tune from a Jewish wedding, tantalising, bittersweet, heated joy with a menacing undertone, with a sense of foreboding. The band came to a standstill right in front of the little white coffin. In the end only one of the violinists continued to play. The clarinet player had put his instrument on the floor beside him. He knelt beside Takuya's coffin. Suddenly I recognised Jochum. He was one of the musicians with whom Ayane had started to rehearse her 'Coupe Maison'. Jochum lifted the little white coffin and put it on the belt by the wall, in which there was a wooden door, a bit like a serving hatch. I suspected the incinerator was behind it. He picked up his instrument again and joined his fellow musicians in a slow, sad melody, heavy with pathos. For a moment I cursed the entire performance, I felt it too slick, too engineered and I felt like screaming, the way our boy would have.

The hatch opened up and the coffin slid inside. The tune had reached its sombre ending.

Upon leaving the auditorium Luc took his wife and daughter by the hand. Swinging from his arm was the plastic bag from which the plush ear protruded.

'Now, daddy,' I heard Tamako say to him. Luc began to free Toby, his daughter's favourite cuddly toy, from the bag. Her face lit up. She kissed Toby's worn out bear face.

'That was a great idea of you, Luc,' I said.
'Yeah?' he sounded insecure. 'It is hard to know what is right for her at the moment.'
'This. What you are doing. Wondering what might calm her down, break the fall.'
'The fall?'
'You know, so much more is happening than a child of four can grasp, don't you feel? And yet she's aware that her world has been shattered.'
During the service I had wondered about these things and how Tamako was going to remember all of this in years to come. Would she remember this day when she turned eighteen? Would she remember more than her brother's name?
'True. I think I'm just trying to keep some normality going.'
'Well, that's the best thing to do.'
'*Merci.*'
'What did you think of the service?'
'Beautiful, beautiful.'

Close up Fumiko was a very attractive woman. It had as much to do with her driven, soulful way of speaking, as with her looks. She had a large, sensual mouth and slender hands, with which she'd gesture suggestively whilst talking, a lot like Ayane did.

'That was very moving, Fumiko.'

'Thank you. Ayane tells me you've written something too, for later?

'Yes. Yes, I have.'

'It will do them good.' I nodded. 'That must have been horrible, out there in Sardinia.'

'Hmm, yes, it was, there are no words for it.'

'No. Can I confide in you, Emma?'

'Yes, of course.' She was not the kind of woman to say no to.

'I'm worried about Luc.'

'Oh.'

'What?'

'You're not alone there.'

'How's that?'

'No, you go first. What was it you wanted to say?'

'He's rung me a few times this week. Both times seriously wasted. I get it though, my sister can't be there for him at the moment, obviously. Those two will have to lick their respective wounds separately, but...'

'But what?'

'I'm not sure, I just get the feeling he's incredibly, I don't know, fragile. And lonely.'

'He is.'

'What did you mean, that you're worried as well?'

'Exactly that. He's sort of absent, you know, far away, not really there. I know it's to be expected, but it's so new, you know, to see him like that. I can't really explain.'

'You're explaining it very well.' I had all her attention. I imagined her to be a good listener.

'Ayane was always the one to take up most of the oxygen in that household, you know? More in harmony with her body and her needs and that. Like you described in your speech, that was so true.' Fumiko just smiled and nodded. 'Luc tends to make himself smaller, perhaps now he hopes that effect will rub off on his misery.'

'Exactly how I see it. Emma, that guy with his BMW?'

'Geert? The man who carried in Takuya's coffin?'

'Yes. Is he a good friend?'

'That's another thing. I'm not sure Luc does the friendship thing. That's more Ayane's terrain. Geert is his tennis buddy, but I think that's about it.'

147

'I'm going to have a little word, perhaps he can help.'

'But you said he rang you, Fumiko? That seems to suggest he wants to open up to you, no? You seem a strong lady and your Ayane's sister.'

'I know, but that's exactly it, it does not feel appropriate somehow.'

'Oh.'

'No, don't get me wrong, I just don't think I'm the right person to help him.'

'I understand.' I did not. Perhaps she wasn't such a good listener after all. Was his grief too much for her? Or was there possibly some sort of attraction?

'Hey, babe.' Ayane was drinking wine. She sounded chipper. 'You want a glass?'

'Why not?' I took a glass from the tray on the table.

'It was a beautiful service, wasn't it?'

'Most certainly. Serene and incredibly moving.'

'With a big dose of Takuya, right?' I thought it was an odd remark, but I did understand what she meant. Today had to be all about him, after all. Shit. He had hardly celebrated one birthday.

'Oh, yes.'

'You ready to speak in a bit?'

'I hope so, yes.'

'You're the only one with an open-air-voice, Emma.'

'Nonsense. And those sisters of yours?'

'Yes, but this is different.'

'How so?'

'You get the last word.' I suddenly realised what that meant; being the last speaker was an honour she had bestowed upon me.

I took the glass from her hand and put it down, together with my own. 'Hey, my wine!' When I hugged her, she held me tight.

'Thank you Ayane, thank you.' She kissed me and held me a while longer.

It was a short drive to the gardens of remembrance.

During the *coffee table* the funeral director had passed round a list to gather the names of all those who wished to come to the cemetery. When we came out, a line of black cars awaited those who needed a ride. Everything was immaculately organised.

I sat in the back of our own car next to Haru. Her twin sat on the other side of her. Hoshi sat in the front next to Raf.
'You have a wonderful voice,' I said to Haru.
At the reception I had not had the chance to talk to her. She seemed to feel at ease with her outsider's role. All by herself in a corner of the room, she had stood and watched the crowd while she took small bites of her roll and sipped her tea. Clearly her friend hadn't come with her.
'Thank you.'
'I hear you live in Brittany? Where about?'
'In Concarneau, in the *Finistère*, the Northwestern bulge on the map, if you like.'
'Beautiful area?'
'Very. Concarneau itself is worth a visit, in fact. The centre of the old town is surrounded by the ancient, medieval walls.'
'Wow. And it's by the sea, right?'
'Yes. It's a natural harbour. Were you Takuya's godmother?'
'Yes.'
She nodded. 'Awful.'
'Yes.'

The parking area next to the cemetery and the Gardens of Remembrance was packed. When we finally found a space and got out, a lot of people from the reception were there already. A bit further afield Ayane and Luc were talking to the funeral director. He was holding a little pot. That had to be Takuya. His little body no longer existed. The lawn was filling with people, as the car park in front of the crematorium had done earlier. Jochum and the two violinists were there too. They were still carrying their instruments. Perhaps that meant there was going to be music here too.
Luc came walking towards me.
'Peter, the funeral director asks if you will be all right without a microphone, Emma.'
'Yes, no problem.'

'When the music stops you can start to speak. Then Aya and I will start to scatter, ok?' Luc's voice was thick with suppressed emotion. I had not seen him cry since we got back from Sardinia.

The musicians began to play. Once again it was an upbeat tune, which sounded familiar. When one of the men took a kazoo to his mouth and started to hum along with the refrain I remembered: it was 'The Bed boat'! An old *Ellie and Rikkert*-song from one of Raf's mother's vinyl records. I had played it for Takuya until its grooves were all but worn out. The song made him go berserk and he never failed to squeal along with the refrain. I could not afford to cry anymore, not now. From the little breast pocket of my dress I took the creased piece of scrap paper, I straitened it. *Fuck, Emma, not now, no bloody weeping.* A woman next to me handed me a paper tissue. I took it from her and pressed it into the corners of my eyes, but it only prompted more fluid. The music stopped. From a distance Luc was staring at me, baffled it seemed. I was ruining his perfect show. 'Sorry', I mouthed, but there wasn't much sound. I cleared my throat and repeated, a little louder. 'Sorry, but this was *The Bedboat*, the favourite song of me and *Takske*. Takuya, I mean.' This was wrong. This was not what you did with an audience. I looked at Ayane, who was nodding courageously, completely dry. 'Go on, Em', her lips said to me. 'Tell him.'

I inhaled the freshness of the wet grass. I found my voice and spoke, though a sheer curtain of soft rain, under a grubby Brueghelian sky and spoke to my godson for one last time.

Takuya
I always liked to say your name
Shout it out loud
Whisper
Or sing it
Tik-Tak-Tik-Tak-Uya
Autumn days in Biessumer-wood
With Tamako and Omoe Hosh
Feeding the goats
Watching the deer
With oma and opa from Gent
In a little red boat

Just you and me
One August day
We sailed the Frisian sea
Ta-kuya!
Repeating your name is all I can do
But words lack the power
To make you real, to make me feel
The singular you
Your perfect round head
Taku-ya!
Your very name
Sums up
What you were
And were going to be
Your mighty promise
We set it free
The force of your being
The spark of your life's begin
We scatter it out there
And claim it within

When I was done Luc and Ayane scattered the content of the urn around them on the grass. I liked it that it was just the two of them. They giggled a bit, when the dust flew back into their direction for a moment. The dust that used to be their baby.

Part 5

Panta rhei
Everything flows

Heraclitus

There was a strong wind. I pushed my bike standing upright, teeth clenched. I did not like using the gears; that felt like cheating. *Como el fuego, el fuego devoradó-ór*, with every revolution the original words of the song came to me. Three days to go to première of 'Land and Water', the production based on a selection of *cantos* from Pablo Nedruda's *Canto General*, which I had adapted and rewritten for children together with Ayane. This year, the spring-celebrations in the city of Antwerp were to reflect the different aspects of Latin American culture and I had been approached for a contribution. It was my most ambitious project since the time I had had my own theatre and was partly subsidised.

After the divorce Raf and I had been able to sell our house for a healthy profit. We'd been able to wipe out our mortgage and were left with enough money each to invest in our respective new homes. It hadn't been a bitter split. At one point, about half a year after we were separated, we'd even once slept together. For a moment we were fooled things could work again. But soon the old irritations resurfaced. He accusing me of being neurotic and bossy. Me finding him somewhat pompous and humourless. Sex together was still as good as it had always been and above all it felt familiar. But we no longer laughed at the same things, if at all and that felt more crucial than ever.

These days we sometimes bumped into one another in town. Raf had had a new girlfriend for two years now. Sandrine was a primary school teacher from Brussels, with two teenage children from a previous marriage. I'd never met her, but he spoke warmly about her and the children. Marie was studying Germanic languages at the University of Antwerp. I was incredibly busy with my theatre work but felt calmer and more fulfilled than I'd ever done.

Ayane's new house was quite a bit further away, a cycle ride of about three quarters of an hour on a busy road, ending with a hefty climb over a viaduct. But I needed the exercise. With the last week's busy rehearsal schedules I had missed both my regular yoga and salsa sessions. The only thing I would not forfeit was my Spanish class on Wednesday nights.

I locked my bike at the gate by the front door and took a bottle of wine from the basket in front of the handle bars. I was early, but then I always was. Luc opened the door, sandwich in hand.

'Hey, Emma.'

'Sorry, you're still eating?'

'Yes, so? You going to be polite suddenly? Come on in, grab a chair. Coffee?'

'Yes, please. Black.'

'Obviously.'

'Hey hon.' I gave Ayane a fleeting kiss on the cheek.

'*Hoi*, Em. You seen Ben?'

'You mean since our last rehearsal?'

'Yes, I thought he was going to hand you a demo of the epilogue, there was something not quite right he said.'

'Bit late for that. Where about? At the very end?'

'He didn't say.'

'I'll give him a ring later.'

'Hey, *Tammeke*.'

'Ta-ma-ko, auntie Em.'

'Sorry. Here, you've not got this one yet, right?' I took a dvd from my bag and handed it to her.

'Wow, cool man!'

'You're spoiling her, Em.'

'Nonsense.'

'How did you like your costume?'

'Awesome.'

Ayane rummaged around in the bowl of biscuits and came up with a handful *speculaas* cookies.

She held out the bowl for me.

'No, thanks. Honestly, you're getting worse then Luc.'

'I know. I blame you. Stress.'

'No, Tam, finish your dinner first, then video.' Luc calmly pushed the girl back in her chair.

'It's not a video.'

'Tamako?' Ayane shot her daughter a reprimanding look.

'Whatever.' I suppressed a smile. The girl wasn't even eight yet but copied all of the gestures and one-liners from her favourite American series. For the moment she was completely obsessed with Hannah Montana. I toyed with the idea of doing something with that on stage next season.

'Can you help daddy clear the table, poppet? After that you can watch your film.'

'Ok' she said, in the same intonation as *whatever*.

'Can you scroll back and show me that other one again?' I moved the cursor to the top of the screen and pressed the blue arrow on the left. I arrived back at the previous website.

'Yes! That's the one. Oh, look, Em, a Jacuzzi.'

'It's very grand, indeed, but a lot less central than the other one.'

'Mmm, pity.'

'Everything ok girls?' Luc kissed his wife lovingly in the neck and stuck his head between ours to look at the laptop. 'Crikey, that's a castle!'

'It is but too far from the centre.'

'What do you call the centre?' he asked.

'The staré město.'

'What?'

'The old town.'

'Right.'

Ayane and I would be going on a city trip to Prague straight after the last performance of 'Land and Water'. Luc would take Tamako camping to Brittany. They had even been invited to stay a few nights with Haru in Concarneau.

In the year after her son's death my friend had not worked. She had let go of her prestigious 'Coupe Maison'. For quite some time it had looked as if Luc and Ayane were not going to make it as a couple. Their inability to communicate or be emotionally present for each other made their marriage a hollow performance, which only retained meaning in the care of their daughter.

One November evening, a little more than three months after Takuya's death, I unexpectedly popped by my friend's house for a visit. As ever, she was lying on the couch in her bath robe and fluffy socks and was drinking red wine from a lemonade glass. The TV was on full blast but she barely seemed to notice. David Attenborough was talking us through one of his quests for rare species in his intriguing, intimate whisper-voice, but it was lost on my good friend. Most things were. At that time I carried a key to her house. Luc often had to work late or arranged it that way and most of the time Ayane would not even bother to answer the door. Tamako spent a lot of time with Hoshi, Luc's mum and dad or with me.

'Aya?' She seemed to find it utterly normal that I was standing in her living room and was switching off her telly.

'What is it?'

'Come here, sit up for a minute.'

'Why? What's the matter?'

'Have you eaten?'

'Yes, of course.'

'What?'

'I don't remember.'

I poured a glass for myself and sat down next to her, lifting her fleeced feet into my lap.

'Honey, listen, we've got some thinking to do.'

'What are you talking about?'

'You.'

'Oh, don't you worry about me, I need a bit of time, that's all.' She stumbled over her words.

'Mmm.'

'What mmm?'

'Ayane, *lieveke*, listen to me. What can I do to help you?'

'What are you talking about?' It was as if I had asked her to dance Swan Lake that same evening.

'How can I help you to move on? What needs to happen?'

'You know damn well what needs to happen.'

'Takuya. Am I right?' His name gave her a shock.

'Emma, what is it you're going to tell me? That that's impossible? Do you really think I'm that simple?' That...that...' Her eyelids drooped. She had drunk at least one bottle of wine and had most likely eaten no more than the packet of crisps.

'Would you like to go to sleep?'

'Sleep, good, yes, in a bed.' I helped her to bed and tried to ring Luc on his mobile, which went straight to answerphone. Tamako would be at her grannie Hoshi's for the rest of the weekend, who would also bring the girl to school on Monday.

I decided to stay over at Ayane's and to sleep on her sofa. The next day was a Sunday. I got up, tidied up the living room and the kitchen, make fresh coffee and toast and scrambled some eggs.

When I entered my friend's bedroom she was hanging out of her bed, retching.

'Oh, Ayane!' I rushed to the en suite bathroom where I found a little plastic tub with bits of soaking laundry, I emptied it in the sink, took a flannel and hurried back to the bed with the empty tub. 'Here.' I held out the tub and wiped her forehead with the wet flannel. When I went to put it down on the bedside cabinet, I noticed a couple of opened packs of paracetamol.

'How many of these have you had?'

'Many.'

'When?'

'Not long ago...'

'Goddamned, Ayane, come on, let's get you to the bathroom!'

I dragged her out of bed. She collapsed on the bath room floor. I pulled her to the bath tub, held back her head with one hand and stuck two fingers of the other in the back of her throat.

'Come on, throw it out, girl, please Aya, throw it all up.'

It was a good thing that Ayane had washed down the tablets with lots of water. Almost immediately she threw up a milky white pulp, in it a whole load of tablets were floating.

'I'm calling an ambulance.'

'No! Please don't. Ten. I took ten.' In a little girl's voice, she went on to confess: 'I wanted to start on the rest but I became unwell.'

I cast my eye back on the milky white mess and made out eight tablets, more or less. 'Come on, lean on me, let's get you back to bed.' To be certain I checked the opened packets. One full strip of eight tablets was empty. From the other pack three tablets were missing. In the worst case she had three tablets left in her system; that wouldn't kill her.

She was leaning heavily into her pillow, her eyes weak and less alive than ever before.

'I'm sorry, Em, I just wanted the pain to go away. I don't want to die.'

'I know, *moppie*, I know.'

Again, I tried Luc's mobile.

'Emma?'

'Fuck you, you fool, why was this thing switched off?'

'Hey, calm down, what's up with you?

'What's up with me? I'll tell you what's up with me: I'm with your wife who's just taken a dozen paracetamols, that's what's up with me!'

'Oh my God! Is she all right?'

'Yes. Luckily, she's thrown everything up, or as good as. She's asleep. What's going on here, Luc? Where are you?'

'I can't take it any more Emma.'

'Oh, yes, that's easy.'

'What would you know about that?'

'What I know is that it is not an option to let her go to hell now, Luc. And if you can't find it in you, or you just don't know how then, fuck, find help! Cowardice is not an option.'

'Excuse me?'

'Sorry, I shouldn't have said that.' It was quiet at the other end.

'Come home, ok?'

'Yes, but it might take a while.'

'What do you mean?'

'I'm in Rotterdam.'

I took her a big glass of Coke and a yoghurt. When she finished it all I tucked her in and lay down beside her. I threw my arm over her.

Just before she dropped off she mumbled: 'Aishiteru, Emu.'

'Me too, Aya. I love you too.'

What is it that makes us change?

Do we lose our dreams along the way? Do we start to make more compromises?

I'd had a short fling with Joris. We'd been to the cinema a couple of times and decided to euphemistically finish the evening with coffee at my place. He was a kind man and an attentive lover and I told myself I was in love with him. But from the very first time it felt as if I was not really there. It was as if I was looking at a scene unfolding, observing it with interest from the sidelines. I was almost more interested in his underwear than in what was inside it. I, who was so very fond of sex, did not feel a thing.

Not long after I was cycling home from my Spanish class. It was a clear, cold December evening, my breath making steaming little clouds in the crispy, frosty air. I was thinking about Victor Jara, the Chilian folksinger, who had been shockingly butchered during the Pinochet putch.
I thought of one of his songs which we had discussed in class. *Ojalà*. Maybe. What a beautiful word that was. 'Maybe I will find roads to travel,' he sang in his kind, warm voice. *Ojalà encuentre caminos.* Such a simple song it was: 'It is hard to find clarity in the darkness, when the sun, which shines down on us, covers up the truth.' What was the truth? Victor Jara had paid with his life for his. I put my bike in the garage, pulled off my boots and went upstairs.
Had the ending of my marriage to Raf less to do with who we were, than with the way we had each lived our story? With unrealised expectations? As I opened the front door the cat wrapped his warm furry body around my legs, purring with contentment.
Hey, Peewee. You ok?' I took off my gloves and stroked his ginger coat. 'I bet you're hungry, Peeps. Tienes hambre, si?' I switched on the light and looked around the place, as if through someone else's eyes. I was pleased with the result. *This room breathes concentrated Em,* Luc had said when he first visited. *Cosy, but not overly manicured.* Behind the screen of the open fire place a few last embers were flickering. I had spent the entire afternoon by the fire, reading on the couch, the cat in my lap. And making phone calls. For over an hour I had bent Ayane's ear about the advantages of a dog that didn't shed hair. Not that she needed much convincing: she'd had her mind set on a Spanish water dog. Luc however was not about to cave in, he wanted a 'Lassie'. Tomorrow Tamako was going to stay over. I looked at the

161

clock: not too late to make her bed with the purple covers she thought were *totally ace*. I planned to take her food shopping first and then prepare a lasagne together. I was looking forward to having her. In the kitchen I opened a tin of cat food. Peewee pressed his little body with more urgency against my shins. 'Cuánto tiempo caminando, desde cuándo caminando?' I sang. In Spanish I felt a different Emma. I was contented. Almost happy.

Had it been a calculated move, demanding of Raf what I knew he wasn't able to give, in order to justify the split? One of the aspects about living on my own I found both satisfying and frustrating was the fact that I could no longer hold another person accountable for my actions. At home, my motives were no longer a response to what was being done to me, or not being done. That way one eliminates quite a few games. But games, whether played by children or adults, make life more colourful. More dangerous, but more exciting too. More complex, but more complete. Spicier. Regardless of how wearing the couple dynamic can be, it offers a context, a theme, a guideline. Fighting, making up or merely ticking over, are pretty much the ebb and flow of living and exploring together. My existence was more straightforward now, more honest, but it was also drier. For the time being, however, it was what I could cope with: *Caminando*, soberly strolling on an untrodden path.

When Ayane came to see me the evening after her overdose, she was fuming.
She had just found out that Luc had been seeking consolation in the arms of Fumiko. Platonic comfort, mind. The physical kind was no longer on offer; that type of relief her successful sister had offered him about eight years earlier. I stood perplexed.

She was sitting at the table of my barely furnished dining room, defiant, arms crossed. I had made chips. We drank beer. Ayane seemed famished.

'He lied, Emma. All those years! Takuya's life was based on a lie.'
'How do you make that out? Aya, that's bullshit.'
'I did not know!'
'Yes, I understand that must be quite a shock and that you're angry but it hardly corrupts the arrival of your children, does it?'
'I did not know, Emma. I hadn't the faintest idea. And now, after all these years, that horny prick has gone sniffing around there *again*.'

'When exactly did you say they were supposed to have had something together?'

'Two days before our wedding! And no, not 'supposed to'. The scheming, hypocritical bitch. I knew she was charmed by him. Fuck.' Ayane sounded livelier, more strident then I'd heard her in months. Was she tapping into an alternative pain, less raw and more tangible, addressable, than the death of her son? She had proper ground now, to be aggrieved.

'But why?'

'Why what? Why was he shagging her on the eve of our wedding?'

'Yes?'

'Search me. Nerves, he says, pre-performance nerves. Flaming idiot.'

'Nerves?'

'Yes, you know, like stage fright. After all this time it turns out that mister of mine is a performer too. Just too much of a coward to face an audience.'

Coward. It was exactly the word I'd slung at him through the phone the other day. But I had not meant it. I hadn't thought him lacking in courage, I'd thrown it out for effect, because I was angry.

'I don't get it.'

'No. Try being in my shoes.'

'But what does he say?'

'That he found my strength threatening, my beauty, my body, my class, blabla blaa, that kind of crap. In other words, it wasn't really his fault he needed to go suck my sister's massive tits, was it?'

'Come on, Ayane, steady.'

'No, it was my fault, you see, my confidence is so threatening, I'm far too comfortable in my own skin.'

'Granted, that is a bit much.'

'Isn't it?'

'Aya?'

'What?'

'Perhaps you won't think this appropriate or even relevant at the minute but, do you still love him?'

'Oh Emma, what do I know? No! Maybe. Yes. The bloody bastard.'

'So, what was he doing in Rotterdam now then? Talking?'

'Yes. Clearing his head, pouring his heart out, crying. With her he can cry, he says. Bravo! See if I care.'

'Of course you do. But can you be sure? I mean that they only talked?'

Ayane nodded.

'How?'

'He swore.'

'And so you believe it?'

'He swore on Takuya's life.'

'I see.' I almost blurted out the obvious: *But Takuya is dead!* 'What will you do?'

'No idea. Fumiko tried ringing me this morning.'

'That's brave of her.'

'Oh yes, let's give her a medal. All those years, Emma, our kids, our lives, this big fat lie.

'And now?' I asked her again. She shrugged her shoulders. 'The poor sod has lost his compass, he says. He has the feeling I won't let him help me. That you're the only one I allow anywhere near me. Fuck, he almost sounded jealous! *He* is jealous!'

'Has he not got a point, a little bit?' Ayane greedily drained her beer glass and pushed her plate aside. She had finished the entire tray of chips on her own.

'I understand your anger, I do. Especially the fact that he never found the courage to talk to you about it. I'd find that hard too. But if there's nothing going on this time, I mean...'

'What? Then all is well?'

'No, not exactly, but in the bigger scheme of things. Is it that important?'

'What is that supposed to mean?'

'Nothing. It's not supposed to mean anything. It's just, so much has happened, Aya. Perhaps it's time you two saw someone. Learn how to talk to one another, I don't know.'

'You mean a shrink?'

'Yes.'

'Get out of here. Anyway, forget it, I'm far too angry to talk.'

'That's a good start, my darling.'

'Oh, shut up.'

'Sorry.'

Sometime later, Luc and Ayane started bereavement counselling. It did more for Ayane than for Luc, who remained adrift for quite a while, rudderless, only to get more stuck in his work. Meanwhile he had climbed the ladder at Flanders Ballet, thanks to some niche digital skill he had specialised in. Even abroad his expertise was in high demand now and so he was often approached to host workshops in major theatres in Berlin, Frankfurt and Vienna.

Even though he was frequently away from home, the time spent together as a family would become increasingly pleasant and Ayane was relieved to report that she and Luc had actually started to talk. The contact with Fumiko had cooled off and would probably never again be what it had been.

Every year on the twenty-ninth of May we marked Takuya's birth with a modest kind of 'Thanksgiving'. Ayane and Luc would invite me for a meal and we'd look at photos and film footage of Takuya and recycle stories in which he featured. During one of these gatherings Tamako had remarked, in all sincerity, why we never came up with new stories.

A year and a half after the death of her son, Ayane started to get more solid ground under her feet. She was beginning to sleep better and had taken up exercise again, still not with an eye on work though. Not that she needed to financially, Luc was earning plenty.

Ayane had become a lot less guarded than she had been. She would more often share a less censored version of events with me. At the same time my friend had lost her gloss and I felt nostalgic for the loss of my naughty, inspired artistic soulmate.

Two years after Takuya's death I was given the sort of opportunity I had always craved. I was rung by the chairman of the Antwerp *Spring Feast* committee with the request to create something with children, fitting the *Latinantwerp* bill.

'But that is wonderful, Emu, congratulations!' my friend said when I rang her with the good news.
'Thanks. I can't quite believe it myself.'
'Oh, my God! That's it, you've made it now.'
'Hold your horses honey, I've not even done anything.'
'Have you got any ideas yet?'
'Yes, I do.'
'What, just like that, straight after their phone call?'
'They rang me two days ago.'
'Oh.' She sounded a bit disappointed. 'I wouldn't have thought you'd be able to keep that to yourself so long.'
'That was hard, you're right. But there was a reason.'
'Oh, now I'm really intrigued. Go on then!'

'I needed time to figure out something I needed your help with.'

'I'm not with you.'

'I want to work with you, Ayane. Truly. A professional pact, the two of us, chipping away at something we both believe in.'

'Oh, my darling, that is terribly sweet, you know, but I'm not sure. I've not done anything for ages. Besides, working with children is not really my thi...'

'Will you just shut up and listen for one minute? You don't even know what I'm going to ask you.'

'Oops.'

'Ok. Are you familiar with the Canto General?'

'Sorry, no.'

'Poems by Neruda? Sung by Mikis Theodorakis and Maria Farantouri, no?'

'No. Don't know it.'

'Doesn't matter. You have heard of Neruda, right?'

'Yes.'

'Ok, well, Neruda wrote the Canto in exile. It's this huge epic tale, tracing the beginnings of the Latin American continent. You know, the oceans, the rivers, the fauna, the flora, but also the heroes of its history, flavoured with folk metaphors and so on. At the same time, it was meant as a call for solidarity with the oppressed. A bit of a Latino-bible if you like, a religious, profane epos, but at the same time a political, militant pamphlet, very ambitious, but very sincere, profound. Canto, by the way, means song, ballad. The Canto General consists of fifteen ballads. At the beginning of the seventies, Mikis Theodorakis, who himself was exiled from a Greece ruled by corrupt colonels, recognised the Canto as a sacred tool of battle for his people and he put it to music.'

'I'm with you.' She sounded tired already.

'Ok, what I would like to try is to transform these cantos, which are essentially poems, for and together with children and weave through it some contemporary themes. These songs are full of images kids can relate to: huge plants and snakes and tigers. Ideal. Obviously, I would not go for such an explicit political theme, but I would want to keep the anti-oppression message, you see? So, I was thinking: what do I need? A structure, a plot, music, but that exists already, well, if I get the permission to adapt it, that is, but I'm sure there's a way round that. And last, but by no means least, a choreography. And ta-da: that's where you come in. So, what do you say?' I was out of breath.

'Jesus Christ, Emma. What are you on?' I began to laugh.

'I must admit I feel slightly high, indeed. And if you say yes now, I am going to go completely bananas. Please Aya, say you'll think about it, at least.'

'But when and how is all of this going to happen, Emma? Just listening to you has worn me out.'

'I have ten months to work out a concept. In about two months' time they need to see a rough draft of the story board. Then I'm given half a year rehearsal time. Although I get the impression they're rather flexible with these blocks of time.' My friend sighed.

'I won't put any pressure on you. If you decide not to join me, I will respect that and try to find someone else. Having said that, there's no one more equipped for this than you and no one I'd rather work with and that's simply the truth. It wouldn't even feel like work.'

'Look, five stars. It's got a courtyard and it's around the corner from the *Church of our Lady before Týn.*'

'I still prefer the other one, Em. Sorry.'

'But we'd be far from everything.'

'So?'

'Listen, do you want to walk for half an hour, three quarters of an hour each night? After a meal and a glass too many?'

'That won't happen.'

'Yea, right.'

'No, honestly. Not a glass too many.' She suddenly sounded very serious. I looked at her.

'Emu, I'm pregnant.' For a long time, we did not say a word. The screen was frozen on the Charles Bridge. Ayane's eyes spoke of fear, hope and wonderment.

'Aya, that's fantastic news, come here.' I grabbed hold of her and kissed her. 'Oh, *lieveke toch*, what does Luc have to say?'

She cast down her eyes in a coy, almost girly fashion. 'He's very, very happy.'

'You sound like the virgin Mary. It wasn't an immaculate conception, was it? Oh shit, you still ok about going to Prague?'

'I'm pregnant, Emma, not ill.'

Ayane and I were standing on either side of the wings, one hand held up. Two respective lines of animals were making their way from the stage towards us, one lot dancing towards *côté cour* the other moving towards *côté jardin*, all had their hands held up, ready to finish off their performance with a bang. It had become our ritual. After the final dance routine, just before the actual finale, we indulged in 'high fives' with all the members of Noah's colourful Ark: iguanas, jaguars, pumas and butterflies came running towards us in their incredible costumes, each with their own trade mark step. Towards the front of the stage, a writhing Tamako sang the last couplet of her snake song.

Deep
Deeper still
In the almighty water
Of the swamp
I
The anaconda
Live
Covered in sacred mud
Wriggling
Writhing
Slithering
Going with
The Flow
As life itself
Covered in sacred mud
As life itself
Devouring and holy

One last slither before she too exited the stage, where her mother awaited her. Their hands met in mid-air.

By my side, Ramirez, a ten-year-old Chilean boy with a voice clear as coral, stood nervously swaying back and forth. I gave him a gentle push. He ran onto the stage and climbed onto the volcano-model. All on his own and without musical support, he started to sing the finale.
A booming applause shook the hall.

Yo no voy a morirme
Salgo ahora
En este día
Lleno de volcanes.

During his final purely sustained note, from all sides children came running onto the stage, long, colourful bandanas on their heads, the colours of all the Latin American countries. When the entire cast had joined him on the stage, Ramirez's voice died down, only to return seconds later, this time supported by the rest of the children's choir. In Dutch this time, they sang the moving last words of the canto.

I will not die
On this day filled with volcanoes
I will choose life
I will stay here
With words and peoples and paths
Awaiting me once again

Londen, Beaumont-du-Périgord
Summer 2012

Acknowledgements

I thank the writer Stefan Hertmans for his unwavering belief in my writing.
I thank Pat Gillen for his honest proofreading sessions.
I thank Dana Peerless for her generous linguistic support.
I thank Dennis Strik, my Dutch editor, for years of patience and for his love of words.
I thank Dr. G.J. Bouma, neurosurgeon, for his kind advice.

ISL Library
020 8992 5823

Printed in Great Britain
by Amazon